HENRI EDSON XIMENEZ

Paul Flum

Published by Conscious Publishing, 2024.

This is a work of fiction. Similarities to real people, places, or events are entirely coincidental.

HENRI EDSON XIMENEZ

First edition. June 17, 2024.

ISBN: 978-1929096152

Written by Paul Flum.

Table of Contents

To Giovanna S.

You And Your Human Defects

———

Here we go again

You cannot accept more from me than memory

You cannot expect more from memory than this

This is this this is nothing else

We've been through this many times so again

A long journey though not the longest

A voyage to pre-experiencing the present

Resorting shuffling the deck

We find you painfully American

So it follows that arriving on its cities shores

Can promote the completion of tasks yes

Moreover a feeling of incompleteness

A pendulum swing of ambivalence and indifference

What could I have done could I have done more

Finding these frontiers as a series of firsts

In this town and in that town

The rest of humanity finds other passions

For example it finds life and death in World Cup soccer

———

2

But as an American you find your joy in identifying

Your unique sports in synch with the jersey you wear

Refusing to acknowledge that your opponent is identical

In words art music literature and culture

They're often leaner

Meaner

And somewhat dumber

Also the eclectic music you invent is

A constantly reshuffled mix tape of your life

This is this this is nothing else

Endlessly documenting a brief history and envious

Of a world who finds you spoiled and tedious

So here we go

Let's test out that memory yet again

Eternal Recurrence

As spotted by the great Friedrich

Look

You don't want to fish around in your wallet

To identify the picture on the drivers license

That matches the mug in the mirror

Is that you?

We're going to rediscover and pre-experience America

With rudder crankshaft and curved scallop wheel-set

This soundtrack clashes with another soundtrack

Solon

He claimed the universe is soundtracks all the way down

What that universe is sitting on is another soundtrack

So here we go this is you

You And Your Human Defects

You are not a person with supernatural abilities

Your perception of sensory events is muddy at best

With no particular sequence coming to mind

Trust me

I would know if you were clairvoyant

Most importantly be mindful

That when we see this and that

That

This

Is not Jesus

No it is not

A Creepy Organ Soundtrack

Let's get started

We are here in your living room

You were napping on a black leather sofa

The southern exposed windows to the left

A cloudy November afternoon in Baltimore

The year is 1997

An old bright top third floor apartment

Fourteen windows to the south plaster hardwood

The non-working fireplace straight ahead

The mantel with assorted knick-knacks including

A Virgin Mary votive candle

A Santa-less snow globe

A broken motorcycle piston

An assortment of rusted iron fittings

And a dried rose

There to the right of the mantel the twenty gallon fish tank

Containing a Red Devil tropical fish

Above it on the wall the poster

From the Metropolis motion picture

On the other side of the mantel a plush chair

On the wall above that a Sonic Youth poster

Yup three guys and a gal with bad intentions

The kitchen is very small

Just enough room for the stove sink fridge

And the 1950s era metal kitchenette table

Yellow daisy pattern without the partition

The missing partition always bugged you

It did then and it does now

You could never find that partition

Stop looking

A pretty bright place southern exposure

Your bedroom is one of three

Also with three windows to the south decorated

The ledge full of hanging plants and flower pots

There are two knotty fig trees situated

On either side of a halfway-filled aquarium

Inside the tank are several frogs hermit crabs

Snails small fish toads an eel and such

The bed desk chair stereo rack crammed in

Strewn about papers without much logic

There is a map with a trip plan indicated

A yellow highlight traced over the interstate route

From Baltimore to New Orleans

The pink highlight shows a route with stops

In Louisville Memphis then to The Big Easy

Inside the desk are guitar picks pocket change

Rubber bands scotch tape stapler paper clips

Old batteries pencil sharpener tape measure

Scissors, blah, blah, blah...

Are you still following this?

Its the usual fare and yes that is fine

Now

Down a long narrow hallway that runs the length

Is the sparsely decorated second bedroom

There is a stereo system with a turntable

Boxes of LP records toolbox cinderblock

More motorcycle parts futon mattress

Various movie and music posters on the walls

One of which the classic Peter Fonda

From Easy Rider yup its Captain America

Bathroom is small tolerable for a couple roommates

Nothing stands out here

Unless you consider a poster of Sid & Nancy

Hanging over the commode as standing out

The third bedroom converted to a music room

Amplifier keyboard tape deck microphones

Various instruments including guitar and basses

A small keyboard drum kit milk crate cables

A philodendron hangs from the center window

Overlooking street lamps on Calvert Street

A 1963 Fender Super Reverb Amplifier

By the looks of it very well taken care of

Go power on the amplifier it emits a gentle hum

A CASIO SK-1 sampler keyboard

Very small and beat-up manufactured

And sold cheap at Kmart in the mid-1980s

Scratched and dented broken keys

Held together with black electrical tape

So power it up tap a few keys

Hear that faint crackle from the speaker?

A TEAC dual cassette deck with mike input

There is a blank tape in one of the trays

Dump the milk crate out on the floor

Those are the instrument patch-cords and so forth

It is an AKAI crystal microphone

It has a quarter inch jack for the cassette deck

Everything connected will play loud and harsh

Keep playing the keyboard

Not quite sure if that will bug the neighbors

The front door opens your roommate enters

Drops motorcycle helmet on the couch

Proceeds to the kitchen

What's going on in the music room?

I heard some rumbling when I came upstairs

I hooked that old CASIO up to the FENDER

And it sounds great! What are you cooking?

Ramen Noodles with a torn packet of green dust

I bet it would sound even better

With that REVERB pedal on

Right so where is it?

It's in my room next to the cinderblock

It is an Ibanez analog delay pedal with reverb

Opening the back the 9 volt battery is missing

In your bedroom a replacement on the desk

You touch it to your tongue

Hasn't anyone told you that you shouldn't do that!

Anyway after the tiny shock

It seems that the battery is practically brand new

Place the battery inside the pedal and click

The pedal and the red light indictor comes on

Connect the reverb pedal to the amplifier

Now the keyboard sounds lush and vibrant

Like a church organ like Phantom

Proceed keep playing the keyboard

Write a bunch of nice little church organ snippets

And record your progress on cassette

Are you losing track of time it's dark now

A crisp Friday evening in early November

Outside the window overlooking Calvert Street

A spider extends its web from the streetlamp

To the live oak outside the window

Place the organ music tape in a walkman

Throw some tapes into a knapsack

Grab your journal typewriter camcorder

Now the question is

Do another Lollapalooza cross country rally?

No because you did that August 1991

Chronicled your drive from Baltimore to Chicago

Then a 52 hour train ride to Seattle

Finally the rental car to Enumclaw

And Jane's Addiction

Fishbone

Violent Femmes

No that idea was worn out

But you just recorded

A Creepy Organ Soundtrack

Did you really? And what visuals will you use?

I think you did and you'll find out

Again I don't know everything

I'm just here to help you remember

The background music for a trip to New Orleans

So climb out the fire escape up to the roof get some air

Sticky tar with a half dozen or so

Non-working chimneys poking through

Now it's dawn Monday morning November 10, 1997

An enthusiastic departure on the roof

Using the camcorder to record shots

Of distant radio towers while in synch

Listening to the organ music on the walkman

Smoke from other building chimneys

The Johns Hopkins University Memorial Stadium

Girders from Sparrows Point

360 degree panorama

The sun arrives fade on TV rooftop antennas

Down the fire escape

An abandoned bird feeder from the summer

The living room window is your fire exit

As a habit one of the few pair of windows

That you have kept free and clear of plants

There is a large 55 gallon tank along the foyer

Filled with auratus and golden mbuna

One wall full of beautiful tropical fish

Even though you are secure on the 3rd floor

You still have two deadbolt locks

This exit faces three other apartments

A charming addition to this one hundred year old

Apartment building is the three story

Spiral staircase and the ornate tile flooring

Who needs an elevator!

On the corner of 30th and Calvert Street

Sits your Eighty Seven Nissan truck burgundy

Front quarter cosmetic damage rocker panel rust

Otherwise high mileage and reliable

You begin The Road To Louisville

Mirror In The Bathroom

———

...20 miles...

...29 miles...

...46 miles...

...75 miles...

...103 miles...

...167 miles...

Hear a noise from the truck and stop

Nothing major probably just rough road

Perhaps control arm CV boot

Also a tick-tick-ticking from the hood

This could be West Virginia or Virginia

Could still be Western Maryland

You really don't care you have some business

To take care of it's the paperwork kind

Here at the rest stop convenience room

These are your conveniences have at it

Coke machine vending water fountain

Ladies to the left

Gents to the right

14

No one is around and I know you're curious

Yep as thought very clean and well kept

Go across the lobby to the appropriate lavatory

While on the can did you hear the door lock?

After your business is concluded

And during the hand washing you spy

The Mirror In The Bathroom

It reveals what appears to be a Red fire door

Behind you

So click that Red handle open and exit

No fire nor alarm

Did you know Nineteen Ninety-One was also Red and

The Minnesota Twins won The World Series?

The Wayside T-Shirt Stand

———

It is Wednesday, August 28, 1991

This place is southeast of Seattle approximately

Five miles from the town of Enumclaw

In your pocket keys to a white GEO metro rental

It is parked right over there

Early morning damp intermittent rain showers

However the forecast is for steady rain later

Some of your belongings in the rental car including

A map to the 1991 Lollapalooza Festival

A Details Magazine with Ice-T on the cover

A tape case knapsack luggage and camcorder

There is an old Ford Econoline Van parked here

Gray not actually gray mostly primer

Someone has painted a giant chucklehead face

On one side of the van with the word

BADMOUTH underneath it

Eli the owner of the van is standing there in front of you

Did they have a raincoat?

A raincoat?

You were checking that convenience store

For a raincoat

Uh no they didn't have a raincoat

Oh well you'll get wet

Hey did you start on that book?

Say I'm halfway through the first chapter thanks

I'm halfway through the first chapter thanks

Whatever man here is the extra ticket

Follow me

Start the car let's follow the van

Place the camcorder on the dashboard

Record this beautiful drive

Crank up the radio

It's playing Ripple written by The Grateful Dead

This version by Jane's Addiction

Traffic starts to slow things up a bit

Stop here in the Lollapalooza Parking Lot

Eli tells you he has to go meet his girlfriend

He will see you later

There are plenty of cars dogs partygoers

Dead heads wanderers

Metal merchants and their ilk dawdling around

There's a small tent to the side of the road

Where a crowd of people seem to be lined up

Not sure what they are buying

You'll remember

Which is good I am happy for you

Happy you purchased a ticket for the event

So that means this ticket from Eli is extra

You see the will call window for concert goers

Ones like you who order over the phone

They give them a phone number

And presto give you the pre-paid tickets

If you are distracted look around a bit more

The small tent is the Wayside T-Shirt Stand

It is actually just a couple of card tables with

Boxes of T-shirts nylon tarp protecting everything

Much needed protection from the heavy rain

There are a couple people handing out things

One is a very pretty young woman

A real cutie

5'5 short wavy hair pale blue eyes

Nice smile wearing a light blue Phillips 66 T-shirt

Hi you look familiar!

So what are you selling?

Shirts are 10 bucks 25 bucks inside the festival

I'll take one you going in later?

No just merchandising it's sold out

The pretty girl cannot get into the sold out concert

Where on earth could she find a ticket?

And three two one

I got an extra ticket

I'll go to will call first to get mine then be back with yours

Wow that would be awesome!

I can't WAIT for you to get back!

Smooth Romeo smooth

On your way examine the ten buck shirt

It is a Lollapalooza Concert T-Shirt Listing 6 bands

Jane's Addiction

Fishbone

Violent Femmes

Ice-T

Butthole Surfers

Siouxie And The Banshees

So collect your ticket from will call and have two of them

Back to the Wayside T-shirt Stand

Wait a minute

The pretty woman has vanished!

Maybe she went in the back

Walk through a cluster of Ponderosa pine trees

Behind the Wayside T-Shirt Stand

Oh you wander around looking for that pretty girl

No-brainer

See that huge redwood tree look closer there is a wooden sign

You can't make out what it says

Tacked to it written in Orange cryptic letters

The Orange paint reveals its brushstrokes

It looks like there is a note or piece of paper

Wedged in between the sign and the tree bark

Whoops...

? ? ?

! ! !

zzzzzzzzzzzZZZZZZZZ...

zzz zzz zz ...

Did you know Nineteen Ninety-Seven was also Orange

And The Florida Marlins won The World Series?

Where is My Mind

———

Well the business was taken care of

Not pretty girl business paper variety

It is now late afternoon on November 10, 1997

Feeling groggy?

Was that a dream?

Well maybe it was but it is time to resume your drive

To Louisville

A beautiful crisp drive through White Sulphur Springs, West Virginia

Wave goodbye to the badlands

New Wave

A train garden landscape in the valley town of Huntington, WV

Only a few more hours of daylight before you make Louisville

The Pixies buzz on the radio to keep you from dozing

Where is my mind

Where is my mind

Where is

My mind

It is dark but you need gas

This station looks closed but the self service gas island is open

Or so it seems

Two of the pumps have notes taped to them indicating

OUT OF ORDER

Check the third pump looks to be functional

Interesting

The gas grades are displayed kind of oddly

PLEASE SELECT GRADE

19Unleaded87octane

19Regular91octane

19Ethanol93octane

20Indigo03octane

This truck knocks could use a boost so lets go high test

Or whatever that says at the bottom

Oh 20Indigo03octane

Indigo

Did you know Two Thousand And Three was also Indigo

And The Florida Marlins won The World Series?

Yes for a second time

Are We There Yet

Here is a nice suburban neighborhood 15 miles north of Baltimore city

The community is called Loch Raven

Standing in front of your rancher style house

Shared with two roommates

The house sits on top of a hill and there are

Twenty or so steps leading up to the front porch

The nickname for the house is Casa Des Arachnid

In lieu of its propensity for spiders

The rest of the street looks like it came straight out of

The TV show I Dream Of Jeannie in that most of these homes

Are ranchers built in the 1960s

There is a park with a lush green across the street

Smells like fresh grass clippings

As Mister Such-And-Such has just mowed his lawn

All blue skies and clouds like cotton balls

You expect Major Nelson or Doctor Bellows

To come bounding out of one of these neighboring houses

In their slippers to collect the evening newspaper

It is June 19, 2003, 5:17 PM

Go inside there is a baby grand piano on the hardwood

Living room floor to the left

The dining room and kitchen with modern appliances to the right

Straight ahead up the stairs are the bedrooms

This house was built in 1967

Up the stairs you spy Jan's bedroom

It's kind of a mess

All the windows have screens

A nice breeze is blowing through the curtains

Her bed isn't made naturally

There is a little spider on the floor

Well

It's got 8 legs it's just sitting there

Leave the little guy alone

Smart

Now find Jan in your bedroom

That's her seated at your computer

Your bedroom doesn't look much different from

The other bedrooms at previous residences

Except all the plants and animals are gone

Jan is cute though you are just friends

What's up?

We gotta move

What? What for?

Yup Jack is selling the house I think your HEX is real

Did you drop off the rent check on time?

Tell her of course you did

Of course I did

Huh whatever I was just starting to get settled in

Speaking of which how long have we been living here?

A blank expression would work

What you forget? It was the end of April why are you acting weird?

I guess this is kind of new to me as well

Well Jack wants us out by October to start listing it

Or Maybe I can talk him out of it

Well good luck

I'm checking apartments on Craigslist now

Hey can you do me a favor?

There's a nasty spider in my bedroom

Could you get rid of it?

Well there he is again

Fast little bugger

On Jan's bed an old copy of SPIN Magazine laying there

On the cover is the rock group REM and the caption reads

Are We There Yet?

Rolled up it might make a good weapon versus spiders

Well it seems our little friend has scurried out the window!

Go through the very bright bathroom

The landlord built a cool glass block wall

Along one side of the shower stall for added light

Look out the bathroom window now

Clouds have rolled in it is starting to drizzle

The spider spins a web from the rosebush to the neighbor's fence

Well

You have something to read and you are next to the commode

Ok I know

It seems like doing a lot of movements and so forth

But it will all work itself out in the end you just have to trust me

This will all make sense one day

Flip through the SPIN magazine

A DO NOT DISTURB sign

Falls out of the spine onto the porcelain

It is a DO NOT DISTURB sign for motels and such

It came out of the magazine insert and says

Property Of The Ohio-Inn

While reading the fine article about the early years of REM

And getting a little business taken care of

Don't forget to glance over to the bathroom door

Maybe Jan's bathrobe had been on the hook before

Covering it up

But there is another one of those Orange plaques

Saw one like that in Washington once

Did you know Nineteen Ninety-Seven was also Orange

And The Florida Marlins won The World Series?

Are you getting the hang of this?

Louisville

It is November 10, 1997

It is late in the evening in your hotel room in Louisville, KY

Actually just outside of Kentucky across the river

In the great state of Ohio

Though I guess you already figured that out

By the looks of that DO NOT DISTURB sign

The rooms are cheaper on this side of the river

You can't remember the last part of the drive

Or not or maybe?

You mull what to do in the AM Churchill Downs?

The gambling barge in the river?

How about neither

The Smith Corona typewriter you brought from Baltimore

To help document your trip it works fine

Before you start typing you don't want to be bothered

Of course you know what to do

Yes place it on the doorknob

And then you can begin typing :

November 7, 1997

27

Extra bedroom...third floor...Charles Village row-house...

I start banging the keyboard...a rather crappy one actually...

It is the Casio SK-1

If connected to a reverb pedal and played through

A vintage Fender Guitar amplifier...well then...nice...man...

That sounds like a church organ...

Pipe organ...Phantom of The Opera...

(bamm bamm)

The downstairs neighbor...complains about the slightest noise...jerk

It is dark...a crisp Friday evening in early November...

Overcast but no rain...heck with the neighbor...

This is a blast...wicked...creepy...

(door opens)

The roommate comes home... drops motorcycle helmet on couch...

I continue playing....

"New keyboard?"

"No the crappy one I pulled out of the pile of junk in the corner...

I tripped it out like a chopper"

"Sweet"

The roommate leaves, and it is time to lay down some tracks

...about 20 of them...forty...forty-five minutes long...

The green beer bottle buzz dwindles...

The music studio closes down...now outside...

A spider extends its web from the streetlamp to

The live oak outside the window

November 8, 1997

I throw some tapes into a knapsack...grab the journal...

Will this be another Lollapalooza cross country rally with camcorder?

Nah...once was enough...it was great in August 1991

Chronicling the drive from Baltimore to Chicago

The 52 hour train ride to Seattle

The rental car to Enumclaw to see Jane's Addiction...

That idea was now worn into the ground similarly like that band

But wait...that creepy organ stuff from last night...

Did I just write a soundtrack? I think so

I dig out the Smith Corona typewriter also

November 10, 1997 - morning

An enthusiastic departure...on the roof...camera on radio towers...

Chimneys...The Johns Hopkins University...Memorial Stadium...

Girders from Sparrows Point...360 degree panorama...

The sun rises fade on TV rooftop antenna...

So

I don't have to point out how messy that all is

As well as your general need for an editor

And also I'd probably ditch the profanity

Or most of it

With that being said you do need some rest

Why?

Because there is a big day coming!

There always is!

zzzzzzzz...... zzzzz.... zzzz...

zzz . . ....zzzz....z..

zzzz...z.z.z.

zzz..... zzzz ... zz...

zzz...z......

zzz..... zzzz ... zz...

zzz...z......

You have awakened on Tuesday

November 11, 1997 7:36 AM

It is time to check out of this hotel do some sightseeing

Record some more video footage to synch with the soundtrack

So where did you park the truck?

Actually the more accurate question is

Where is the truck parked?

Now at The Ohio Inn Checkout Counter

Drop the motel key off and get receipt

Ahh how clever your assigned parking spot printed right there

These walls are full of brochures

Filled with exciting things to do in Louisville

The one on the counter is very interesting

Christ Church is the oldest church building in Louisville

Founded May 31, 1822 when Louisville was a bustling town

On the western frontier

This congregation still in its original location

Is today a vital presence in the center

Of the modern City Of Louisville

The truck has a fine cold start

Ok I think we're going to Euclid street

And then off of Washington Avenue

And then I'm not sure

I don't know this building

I don't know this street

For this to work I need you

Well you need you

To pull your own weight

Get us driving get this driving done

See

There is a cool building

Stop the truck here in front

It is actually an old church

Not the one in the brochure

Though it is still a pretty nice piece of architecture

It is called Church Of The Holy Name

There is a Beautiful Archway here

Walk up the church steps stained glass-like tile

Nicer than the tile in your apartment spiral staircase

Of course

The name etched in the archway above the doors

This would make an excellent photo opportunity

As you need to get cracking on that soundtrack

Black & White would capture the moment here

Synch up the music from the walkman to the camcorder

Start recording in Black & White

Louisville was never going to be a big part of the trip

Just a hub and a motel

Are you getting anxious about what continues down the trail?

Hopefully making it to Memphis before sundown

It is a familiar case too many miles too little time

What could I have done could I have done more

Hmmm I heard that somewhere

Anyway

November 11, 1997, 9:52 AM

It is time to head to Memphis, Tennessee

Would like to get there in time to catch the sunset

So you better step on it

Punch it!

Memphis

...21 miles...

...67 miles...

...101 miles...

...185 miles...

...233 miles...damn this truck gets GREAT gas mileage

...301 miles...I spoke too soon

Needless to say a stop for gas

No need to bore you with the details this time

As you top it off without an Indigo Incident

...358 miles...

Graceland

Sun Records

Memphis, Tennessee!

Home of Danny Thomas Parkway and The Pyramid

The Mississippi River is to the west

November 11, 1997 it is late afternoon

Sure you may be looking for Elvis and Johnny

Otis and Booker

Though it is kind of late in the day for that sort of thing

Check those places out tomorrow instead

As the glow of dusk meets the garnet sky

It's time for some shots with the camera before it gets too dark

A drive towards the Mississippi River

Look north spot that enormous flock of blackbirds

Ravens crows can't really tell

They're heading for some power lines

An unnamed Tennessee-Arkansas Park

Well the park sits smack underneath the interstate bridge

Connecting Tennessee to Arkansas

Driving around a bit in the distance

What looks like it could be an incinerator is burning

Fiery blasts shooting through the sky

Best to keep moving while the sun still lingers

Now the fiery blasts appear to be a power station

Where the birds landed

Lots and lots of blackbirds here

Wow

Hundreds of blackbirds are perched

On the electrical cables scaffolding

Various piping conduits a clothesline of crows

I wouldn't want to be the guy in charge

Of scraping off and mopping and such

Blackbirds everywhere straight out of Hitchcock

Shoot this and do it so the birds are white

And the background is black

They seem pretty chill anyway like they're posing

Synch up the music from the walkman to the camcorder

And select the negative filter

Presto

A recording of Birds On A Wire

The street lights for the Mississippi River Bridge go on

That same motel trick will probably work again

The one where you leave the populous town

And cross the state border for a smaller price

Darkness has fallen the first motel will do

In this case Motel Arkansemphis

Check in the clerk will put you in room 04

While in the lobby snag a free city paper

The Memphis City paper

Let's see what is happening

The entertainment section and yes it is happening

Entertainment November 12, 1997 8:00 PM

Link Wray and the Wraymen

Automatic Slims

10 bucks

That date is tomorrow which also happens to be

Your birthday

Trust me

You don't have to pull out your drivers license to verify that

Leave the check out counter and get settled into your room

I see a bounce in your step yes Link Wray man

Cool

Tomorrow

Wait a minute

What kind of a motel has numbers that start with a zero?

I mean 04?

There is masking tape covering up part of the key to room 04

04

When you rip off the tape it now reveals

20Violet04

Violet

Did you know Two Thousand And Four was also Violet

And The Boston Red Sox won The World Series?

Octoberiffic

Downtown, Baltimore

In the Mt Vernon area to be more exact

In front of your apartment building

There is a first floor business office to the left

A messenger company owns it

A staircase to the apartments straight ahead

It is October 13, 2004 11:02 PM

Climb the steps to the third floor single bedroom apartment

The dreaded Mt Vernon Apartment

The living room overlooks Charles Street

The small eat-in kitchen is kind of pointless

Just flick the switch and watch the cockroach race

So safely dart to the bedroom

There is your bed desk projector stereo equipment

Windows to the west and shower to the northwest

Your desk organizational skills have clearly waned

What is it about messy desks?

Does it incite the inquisitive mind?

To find the idea within Chaos?

Would Plato approve?

On this desk we do find

A tattered notebook with loose type-written pages inside

Yellowed and bounded together

Here a bookmark lies absently with some scribbling on the back

The computer is on and there is a message on the screen

We have a cutout newspaper clipping and scissors

Half a glass of some dark beverage and more blah, blah, blah

The PC appears to have a transcript from an MSN Messenger chat on

Oh this is interesting

In the desk-jet printer tray is a copy of that same chat

It must have been important to print it out so here we go :

> *10/13/2004 10:42:33 PM you Octoberiffic and watched Bottle Rocket*
>
> *(Wes Anderson) over the weekend*
>
> *10/13/2004 10:42:56 PM you Octoberiffic and Swimming with Sharks*
>
> *(Kevin Spacey)*
>
> *10/13/2004 10:43:08 PM you Octoberiffic that's why I'm SO*
>
> *BUSY!!!!!!!!!!!!!!!!!!!!!!!!!*
>
> *10/13/2004 10:43:15 PM you Octoberiffic ;)*

> *10/13/2004 10:43:55 PM you Octoberiffic and I saw the latest*
>
> *John Waters film*

40

last Friday at The Rotunda

10/13/2004 10:45:16 PM Octoberiffic you ??????????????

10/13/2004 10:45:35 PM Octoberiffic you jeez

10/13/2004 10:45:38 PM your Octoberiffic A Dirty Shame with

Tracy Uhlmann

10/13/2004 10:45:45 PM you Octoberiffic didn't like it

10/13/2004 10:45:53 PM you Octoberiffic fell asleep to it

10/13/2004 10:46:05 PM Octoberiffic you I've pretty much lost my tan

10/13/2004 10:46:19 PM Octoberiffic you Tracy doesn't do much for me

10/13/2004 10:51:51 PM you Octoberiffic u like short stories?

10/13/2004 10:53:48 PM Octoberiffic you yes

10/13/2004 10:54:10 PM you Octoberiffic I'm writing one for ya....

Something 'bout A HEX...two parts a BOOK ONE and BOOK TWO

10/13/2004 10:54:14 PM you Octoberiffic email it

10/13/2004 10:54:36 PM you Octoberiffic well, I gotta get BUSY then...

10/13/2004 10:54:42 PM you Octoberiffic oh I like the pic of you

in the blue Phillips 66 T-shirt!

10/13/2004 10:54:57 PM you Octoberiffic l8tr tater

10/13/2004 10:56:59 PM Octoberiffic you oh yeah?

10/13/2004 10:57:14 PM Octoberiffic you then it'll be a true story

10/13/2004 10.57.24 PM Octoberiffic you I love that shirt

Its for getting my feet wet on the beach

10/13/2004 10:57:43 PM you Octoberiffic okie dokie

10/13/2004 10:58:03 PM you Octoberiffic but first a beverage

10/13/2004 10:58:20 PM Octoberiffic you beer?

10/13/2004 10:58:24 PM you Octoberiffic ummm

10/13/2004 10:58:33 PM you Octoberiffic there's one left in the fridge

10/13/2004 10:58:41 PM you Octoberiffic I'll have to go sloooowww

10/13/2004 10:59:30 PM octoberiffic you that's enuff

WNDRGRL

over and out

Come on now

I can appreciate the general silliness here but

That salutation

Doesn't it bring some levity to the situation?

Right?

It must or it wouldn't be documented on printer paper

Show some joy!

Come on man show some!

Ilsa Navas

———

The newspaper article comes from the business journal

It was neatly cut out with unsharpened scissors

Actually

More digging around on the desk reveals many more clippings

All from the same journalist

This particular one sits most prominently

The author is contributing writer Ilsa Navas

And she writes :

My meeting with Raissa spurred by her artist statement

That for ten years she has been inspired by

The chicken

A representation of the dualities of life

Absurd beautiful funny yet tragic

They bring hope and carry shadows

I would discover this in her exhibit

At The Mary Jelenfy Gallery

This collection depicts a study of Madonna and Child

Who also embody dualities of joy and tragedy

In her biography Raissa states she grew up Catholic

In New Mexico with all of these images

Sensual Spiritual Ephemeral Timeless

Then in Europe the Black Madonna of Czestochowa

The dense layered indigenous traditions

Later she goes on to Italy

Inspired by Bellini Titian Tiepolo

The extravagance of Venice churches

It culminates with Raissa at her work at San Ysidro

Bridging Mexican and European Catholicism

I was struck that at this exhibit

Here in downtown Baltimore

Her re-imagining the historical use of

Goldfinch and Sparrow

To the dove in Madonna and Child imagery

And in her extension

This chicken takes these depictions further

What is your belief?

The light and shadow in these works

Demonstrates hers

Won't you please come?

And learn more about yourself?

Her work will be up through November 1st

—Ilsa Navas

The Tattered Notebook

———

Let's take a look at this notebook

The bulk of it is tattered and yellowed with inconsistent aging

The font in use looks similar to that

Of a Smith Corona Typewriter :

November 10, 1997 - afternoon

...a beautiful crisp drive through White Sulphur Springs, West Virginia...

I'm 'waving goodbye' to the badlands...a train garden landscape near Huntington...

only a few more hours of daylight before Louisville...

The 'Pixies' buzz on the radio to stay awake...

where is my mind...where is my mind...

July 19, 2003 - afternoon

A rancher style house in the suburbs...in a beautiful cul-de-sac...

straight out of "I Dream Of Jeannie" with Major Nelson and Dr. Bellows...

I come home and Jan is on my computer...

"What's up?"

"We gotta move"

"What? What for?"

"Yup...Jack's selling the house....I think yr HEX is real"

...they sit there and discuss their future...

a spider spins a web from a rosebush to the screen door...it starts to rain...

November 10, 1997 - evening

It is now evening at the motel in Louisville, KY...

actually just outside of Kentucky across the river in Ohio...the rooms are cheaper

I mull Churchill downs in the AM...or perhaps the gambling barge in the river...

it will be neither...I pull out the typewriter and begins this...then sleep...and then...

November 11, 1997 - morning

I check out of the cheap motel...what isn't a cheap motel?

I need a church...creepier the better...the organ music cassette walkman

can be synched to the camcorder to record

I find the right church in black & white...

November 11, 1997 - afternoon

Memphis, Tennessee...looking for Elvis...Johnny Cash...

I settle for an incinerator... fiery blasts in the dim sunset...

birds swarming a power station...

the street lights on the Mississippi River bridge go on...

soon I'll try the motel trick...this time it's Arkansas...and a cheap room...

It continues on like that with missing time sequences

Let's keep looking on the desk

The last thing of interest is a cardboard bookmark

Usually these paper kind get tossed

For some reason the frayed dog-eared nature of this card

Kept it noted guarded protected

The front of it is stamped with the Louie's Bookstore and Cafe logo

A Baltimore institution of the well read

But the real sparkle on this bookmark

Lies in what is written on the back :

Hey

I will be at Louie's Bookstore reading cards on Thursday

Let me know if you're coming

We can meet early to do yours

I cannot believe Gore lost!

This inauguration is going to be a blast

At least that's what the Tarot says

Mea Culpa

Mortal Arthur

There is some other indiscernible scribbling

Beneath the moniker of the cheeky Mortal Arthur signature

Sounds like quite the fellow

OK

Shut the computer down and turn the desk lamp off

Dump out the glass of brown beverage in the sink

It has been a long day

With a long day of reading both then and now

A lot of information to take in

Not a bad time to go grab yourself a bath and call it a day

Nothing like a long hot shower to relax

Turn the knob for cold first or you will get scorched

Oh so the hot water knob is a bit stuck?

Keep cranking on the big Orange knob

Otherwise you will catch a cold shower instead

Finally you break the hot water grip

When turning the hot water knob 180 degrees clockwise

The ON spells NO

As in The Big NO

Did you know Nineteen Ninety-Seven was also Orange

And The Florida Marlins won The World Series?

Uh huh

You are starting to catch ON

Jackson Square

November 12, 1997 1:47 PM

In the French Quarter of New Orleans, Louisiana

The area known as Jackson Square

It is your birthday

It is a balmy and partly cloudy day

Vaguely recall being in Memphis?

Did you stick around long enough for the Link Wray show?

I guess not because here we are

Maybe you assume Link will play here in a few days?

He won't

Perhaps you simply fell asleep in that Arkansas motel room

And forgot all about it

Anyway

One of the goals of this trip was achieved

When departing Baltimore on Monday morning

That is to make it to New Orleans in time for your birthday

To have your Tarot read

There is of course plenty to see and do here in The Big Easy

There are countless street performers

Scads of musicians playing various brass-wind instruments

Percussionists string fellows with their conductors

Horse drawn carriages balloons the smell of fried dough

Dennis Hopper leaving a brothel

OK

Got a little carried away at the end there

Stick with me though

You have inspected the camcorder to find that

The RED led battery is dead

You need to find a place to recharge your batteries

There are plenty of people having their cards read

Let's wait a little bit for the line to go down

To the north are the many bars of Bourbon street

Then Louis Armstrong Park

Beyond there a cemetery

Onto historic Bourbon Street I suppose

There is plenty of drinking on tap

The Blues On Bourbon Street will have to do

As the first bar you spot

So stroll in feeling a bit thirsty a tad parched

Since it is the afternoon not as crowded

I guess all the tourists are outside soaking up the nice weather

No bartender currently up so you scout out the tables

A small table by the window will work

It has a red and white checkered tablecloth covering it

Drop your gear here wait and hope

That the bartender gets back soon

Alas the mustache in apron approaches

What will it be?

Something simple we'll need a favor from him in a bit

How 'bout a bud?

We have bud wanna start a tab?

Sure nothing I like better than drinking and driving!

No expression

I'll just settle up thanks

You have a bud

Curb the sarcasm next time

Now glance under the table there is an AC outlet

The tablecloth hung low which is why you didn't see it initially

The camcorder is plugged into the AC outlet

And the battery is recharging

You'll have to leave the camcorder on the floor

Near the outlet if you wish to walk about

I guess you could leave it here to recharge

But let's check with the bartender first

What will it be this time?

Skip the banter go straight to the camcorder question

Hey would it be OK if I left my camcorder under that table

Look I'm not responsible for other peoples valuables

I hear you

Look kid why don't you just give it to me

It can recharge here behind the bar

Oh great thanks!

See asking for permission is easier than forgiveness

Not going to turn that maxim around?

Never mind

Exit and target the southwest end of Jackson Square

There are several tables of gypsies fortune tellers malachite rock-hounds

There is even a gentleman who can take just one look at your shoes

And bet you five bucks that he knows where you got them

And of course

Tarot card readers

So yes you missed Link Wray but this chick can read your cards

Priorities

Go ahead don't knock over the crystal ball

She will say

You will move away from home sometime

In the next six months

It will be 100 miles from home

Wow nice she is good

But I am better

Don't you think?

The ingratitude to be unappreciated in ones own lifetime

I'm helping man

Next

Feeling uneasy about the reading?

There is still plenty to do

Think

The camcorder battery is probably charged by now

Its getting late in the afternoon

The mission is still that soundtrack and times wasting

You'll want to do more sightseeing

Let's get back to the Blues on Bourbon

The chatty bartender is gone

Now there is an old wrinkled bartender with an eye patch

The eye socket

It would scream like a banshee when the trade winds blew!

Or overheard something like that

He appears now as a cantankerous ol' cuss

A wacky ol' nutbag as it were

What would it be this wonderful afternoon young man?

Hello is the other bartender here?

What other bartender?

Maybe you can help

I left my camcorder here is it behind the bar?

Let me check

Thanks

He's checking

Ok lets see

Do you remember riding in a horse-drawn carriage?

You didn't

Do you remember beignets and black coffee at Cafe Du Monde?

You didn't

Just killing time

He's still checking

Checking

Ah here he comes now

Is this it?

That be the one! Thanks

He hands you the camcorder

Check the GREEN indicator light and see it is fully charged

Let's get down to Louis Armstrong Park

There is a wonderful garden there

It's just four blocks or so from Bourbon Street

At Rampart Street

It has bridges covered with vines and streams throughout

This park made of grassy knolls and lagoons

It is named after the New Orleans native

Even though he was not allowed to play here

In the now well-known clubs during his career

Maybe you can find some kind of nature

To capture with moving pictures

Various types of ground covering type plants

Pachysandra

With a whole kaleidoscope of colors

A great photo opportunity perhaps

Embellish this shot by blurring the image

Bring up the color highlights while changing the contrast

Synch up the walkman to the camcorder

Saturate and solarize posterize

And record the lovely flower fauna and foliage

Maybe you should check out the cemetery some other time

Somewhere in this park is supposed to be

A statue of the great Louis Armstrong

As you jaywalk across Rampart Street

A young woman driving a 1967 Mercury Cougar

With Washington State vanity tags

WNDRGRL

Almost runs you off the road

Now on the ground in the middle of the street

A little dinged up and shaken

Take an inventory to see that

All body parts are working fine

Dazed stand up and look around

A small ticket stub

And a folded up piece of loose-leaf paper

Are lying on the ground

Perhaps they fell out of your shirt pocket

Here is what the loose-leaf note says :

Hey,

I'm writing this because I didn't want to wake you. My train stop is 3:15 AM

in Pocatello, Idaho so my dad already left The Snake River and is meeting me.

We're going whitewater rafting tomorrow! Anyway, you asked me for a list of
things

to do when you get back to Chicago next Saturday...

I would say go to Medusa's.

It is always big on the weekends.

It has a lot of cool rooms in it you might get lost!

Well, have a great time at Lollapalooza, wish I was going with you.

It was great meeting you

and I hope we can stay in touch.

Love,

Heide

And now a closer look at that Red ticket stub :

AMTRAK TRAIN 0387 EMPIRE BUILDER

LEAV SEATTLE AUG 29 1991 805 AM

ARRV CHICAGO AUG 31 1991 213 PM

THIS IS YOUR BAGGAGE CLAIM NO. Q3Z1241

Did you know Nineteen Ninety-One was also Red

And The Minnesota Twins won The World Series?

Yes you should by now

Medusa's

———

Ask any stuntman

The near miss is probably the scariest of all stunts

They would much prefer the high speed crash

Those are more common in Hollywood productions

The stuntmen can prepare their rigs for the collision

They understand the G forces and load speeds

For safety purposes

But the near miss is exactly what it is

Precision

Logic geometry physics

Recalibration

Any mistake erring in either direction

Endangers lives or delays the production

You probably thought none of that

As you dust yourself off on Rampart street

Looking up and here is the North End Parking garage

Whoa this doesn't look like Louis Armstrong Park anymore

Turn around and well yes

This is indeed the Chicago Union Station

Travel By Train

Are you hallucinating is that a train station?

What happened to the French Quarter?

Climb the stairs and enter the Great Hall of Chicago Union Station

Check the date and time on the big clock

It is Saturday August 31, 1991 5:56 PM

This beautiful hall has an enormous skylight atrium

Dozens of long wooden benches for the thousands

Of commuters who pass through each day

The ticketing check-in and boarding are on this level

The baggage claim is down the escalator below

That ticket in your pocket could be put to some use

Here in the baggage claim office of Union Station

Quanidra is the clerk on duty checking tickets

An exchange of ticket stub

Brings you one blue hard-shell American Tourister suitcase

The stub and note were both in your pocket

And by the tone of Heide's note she suggested going clubbing

At Medusa's

Surely you'll recognize one of your vehicles parked here

In the North End Parking garage

You parked a vehicle here a week earlier

Before boarding the train to Seattle and Lollapalooza

There is an elevator to help you find the vehicle

If you can only remember where you parked it

If you are still stumped consider a Maryland license plate

Clicking the button to summon the elevator

As no MD tags on the first floor

The third floor that rings a bell

Hmmm maybe up one more level

Damn

OK lets check the third floor again

Now you just set the alarm off on a Saab 900S turbo

You really could have owned that?

You really could have afforded that?

On your budget?

OK lets check the third floor one more time

My guess is that there is a Toyota key in your pocket

Ah finally

It is your black 1980 Toyota Corolla hatchback

Kicking Alpine stereo

Runs like well it runs like it made it to Chicago

Toss the suitcase in the backseat

And look for some info to locate

The club Heide mentioned in her note

Aha spy a news stand with free weeklies

A vast assortment of maps magazines newspapers and so forth

Here is a copy of The Chicago Reader

It should have an entertainment section listing off all the hip clubs

ENTERTAINMENT : Clubs are sorted by letter

K - O

Katerina's 1920 W. Irving Park

Liar's Club 1665 W. Fullerton

Martyrs' 3855 N. Lincoln

Met USA 3730 N. Clark

Mix 2843 N. Halsted

Nick's 1516 N. Milwaukee

Hmmm not what we're looking for

This might take a little bit more investigation

Try this

ENTERTAINMENT : Clubs are sorted by letter

A - E

Abbey Pub 3420 W. Grace

Andy's 11 E. Hubbard

Bar Vertigo 853 N. Western

Black Beetle 2532 W. Chicago

Club Medusa 1824 W. Augusta

Darkroom 2210 W. Chicago

There you go Mister Navigator

1824 W Augusta

It's about a half hour drive from the train station

Let's see how the Corolla cold starts

After a week of dust accumulates on the hood

Fires right up

Three quarts of 10W40 on passenger floor mat

Just in case

Now it is August 31, 1991 8:03 PM

The drive to Club Medusa goes smoothly

The Club Medusa (or Medusa's) is a big two story rock venue

It looks like someone converted an old rickety house into a club

Standing in front within a synthetic cloud of second hand smoke

A small group of people are getting carded in front of you

Climb the six steps leading up to the foyer

The front hall after this entrance is called The Bauhaus Room

It is very dark

Actually it is very black

Actually it is all black

Well it is painted black

Must be a reason other than that Stones song

There are purple fluorescent light fixtures at the base of the wall

Illuminating tiny swirly dust particles over a black velvet curtain

Intentional maybe

Apparently converting living dining bedroom closet areas

Creates something for everyone as the droves pile in

Flack-kneed proletariats burghers denizens the whole lot

A convention of Ministry and Wax Trax Records T-shirts

Towards the right looks like a small cubby hole

Seems to lead to a closet or some type of coat check room

Now this is the Krooked Stairwell as it is called

As all these rooms are named following protocol of the club design

Twisting at the bottom the stairwell lights at the top folding popping

Then arriving at The Red Velvet Room

There is a small bar here with a bunch of folks gathered around

A jukebox is in the corner and plays at a moderate level

So the folks can hear each other

The wall directly ahead has the red velvet curtain covering it

A beanbag chair ignored and out of place

A hallway to the south where there seems to be vibrating walls

Here we have The Country and Blues Palace

This appears to be a concert hall with acoustic drama

There is a small stage a few tables with candles on them

The PA system is playing a mix tape

There is a band on stage setting up their instruments

Surprisingly this room is decently lit

Let's continue the investigation

We find The Wardrobe-A-Rama

Looks like this used to be a spare bedroom at one time

A single 40 watt light bulb hangs from the ceiling

There is a rather large open wardrobe with coats hung

A rather bored looking coat check person storing garments

In the wardrobe on the floor and on clothing display racks

Which were probably stolen from a Woolsworth or Value Village

Not much at all let's keep moving to The Nitzer Front 242 room

A very loud room industrial music is playing people dancing

A strobe light and disco ball very crowded

A man screams

Hey poor you don't have to be poor anymore

Jesus is here

The proletariats raise their fists in mock solidarity

Too much noise not our scene let's bolt to the next room

Oh my they call this one Mirror Mirror Mirror

Yup you are in a room full of mirrors

As soon as you enter the room you left

Got strangely quiet weird

When you look ahead and approach it is a loud industrial room

Or techno wait

Was that the room you were just in?

Pointless to have two techno or industrial rooms

Ok maybe we are out of our element a bit

Next

This area is called Last Chance on the Stairwell

Unlike the Krooked Stairwell

A long hallway dark not painted black just dark

Colder

It is nighttime and there are no electric lights present

The room is lit by a window without a curtain

Oh actually all other windows are covered by black curtains

That explains the colder

A missing wall

Mental note don't visit this place in the winter

Here

An outside streetlamp

With spider web extending to chain link fence

It is much cooler in this room at the end of the hall

You see an open window and another staircase

That leads to the outside of the club

Which frankly is a good place to be

Not as bumping like she described

Oh maybe the underage crowd vacates soon

After all that I think we're too early

That is a lot to take in maybe come back later

Apparently things don't start hopping till after midnight

Time to pivot

So a motel dinner shower change of clothes

Investigate the contents of the blue American Tourister

Who knows what you will find?

Fifty Two hours on a train from Seattle

And even the black clad denizens of Club Medusa

Wouldn't respond kindly to your club car stench

Now it is after midnight

September 1, 1991 midnight

Returning to Medusa's park the Toyota

You discover just down the street a ways

Dipsy Doodle's Gift Bazaar

It's a gift shop now was once probably a failed auto garage

The front entrance is through a roll-top door which is up

Customers are milling about

Many displays of lawn ornaments and other outdoor doohickeys

Multiple Ikea shelving units with dozens of plaster statues arranged

Gargoyles gnomes demon faced creatures all unpainted

An umbrella stand napkin holders wheelbarrow bird feeders

There doesn't seem to be much of a theme to this place

How about a souvenir?

Something small enough for the Toyota

A small gargoyle statue a foot tall and sixteen inches wide

A menacing dog or demon faced creature with a chain around its neck

Feet which look part paw part talon

It is completely unpainted unfinished white alabaster or plaster

Grabbing the gargoyle you knock over a pitcher of orange juice

Which of course explodes on the concrete

And Orange is everywhere

Orange

Speaking of Orange

Did you know Nineteen Ninety-Seven was also Orange

And The Florida Marlins won The World Series?

But the club?

What club?

Did you say you wanted to go back to the club?

Saint Louis Cemetery Number One

Whew... What was she doing?

She could have run you over!

A close call that left you delirious for a few moments

A near miss

It is November 12, 1997 4:37 PM Louis Armstrong Park

Check your shirt pocket

No note

Check again

No baggage claim tag

Damn

Further down the street we can now see

Saint Louis Cemetery Number One

One of many cemeteries where the dead are buried above ground

In open vaults so many people are buried here

Finding the walls of the cemetery to be their final resting place

Hundreds of people stuck in the walls

Stuck in the middle with you

Burial in the ground was frequently a soggy affair

Since much of the city lies below sea level

The wet rotting corpses were believed to be responsible

For outbreaks of a number of diseases including

Dengue fever

Typhoid

Malaria

Yellow fever

The cemeteries have been in use for over 200 years

And are still being used today

Newer tombs are shiny marble

Some soar 20 to 30 feet high with room for

Generations of family members plus elaborate reliefs

Older ones are decaying brick covered with plaster

In a few cases these older tombs have been maintained

Through a perpetual trust or they are restored

Through the efforts of local preservationists

Very often the original graves have completely disintegrated

Leaving only a stone slab

A pile of rubble

And brick

And a rusting cross to mark the place

Where someone's loved one is buried

There is a tour going on but stay far away for privacy

This is not a good place to visit at night either

Because real life ghouls can

Hide in the cemetery and wait

For their unsuspecting prey to arrive!

No one can see or hear your cries for help from the street

It is several hours until sunset so it seems safe

You saunter by a tomb

It is 15 feet tall by 10 feet square

A black wrought iron fence surrounds it about waist high

Imbedded into the marble where the casket would be

Is a cast-iron face of a lion

As you slowly pan up

It is a statue of the Virgin Mary

However the head of the statue has been destroyed

You recall seeing this same tomb

In the motion picture Easy Rider

Near the end of the film

Captain America Peter Fonda placed his arm around the statue

Obviously before the head was missing

And begins weeping

Captain didn't find what he was looking for

This is a rare and fantastic camera opportunity

Use a filter that gives it an aged quality

With walkman and camcorder and using a slow pan

A recording of the old statue with the missing head

Nearby

A stone slab or the rubble that is left of a tomb

There are crumbled pieces of red brick and marble strewn about

Some of the smaller pieces have fallen off

They are just laying in the pathway of the cemetery

The name "J. A. Rousseau" is noted here

As you explore the stone slab you see a single piece of marble

Six inches long and two by two inches wide

Could be of alabaster or marble maybe not

More likely granite or limestone

It is laying at your feet

And is small enough to fit in your knapsack

Oh and the tour group is gone

And there is nobody looking

I set this all up perfectly for you

So

Do you want to take the brick or not?

Yes?

Are you SURE you want to take the brick?

Yes you think so?

Even if by taking the brick you are basically desecrating a gravesite?

I don't care I want the god-damn brick!

Well

So glad to see you discover a voice

Alright just so we're clear here

You remember

We have been through this many times before

And you just don't seem to remember

You cannot expect more from memory than this

You cannot accept more from me than memory

You now possess the brick

It is in your knapsack

The same knapsack that appears to be dripping

You hear the footsteps of the tour guide approaching

Dripping red

Red

That's not blood?

Is it?

Did you know Nineteen Ninety-One was also Red and

The Minnesota Twins won The World Series?

Blood Red

The Chi-Sox

September 1, 1991 12:37 PM Windy City

What a night

Do you recall returning to Medusa's and getting hammered?

Getting fairly queasy in the Mirror Mirror Mirror room?

Punching up Patsy Cline on the Juke at Red Velvet?

And seducing Vampira in the Bauhaus club?

Or was that in the Nitzer Front Techno doo-dab room?

Anyway

Bloody Mary brunch and mojitos to work off the hangover

Sunday afternoon the weather is beautiful

It would be a great day to relax sit in the sun

Melt off the last bits of the hangover

Take a gander again at The Chicago Reader

SPORTS

Football

Minnesota Vikings at Chicago Bears Soldier Field SOLD OUT

Baseball

Chicago Cubs at Los Angeles Dodgers 7:00 PM WGN-TV

Cleveland Indians at Chicago White Sox Comiskey Park 2:00PM

Plenty of seats still available

Bingo

It is off to Comiskey Park

The plan is ticket left field bleachers bake in the sun

Perfect

The bleachers of what is The New Comiskey Park

This ballpark replaces The Old Comiskey Park

Which lies in torn down bricks and rubble across the street

Hmmm rubble and bricks again

It is a glorious day an Oakley sun bath

The home team White Sox AKA The Chi-Sox have

Just finished batting in the third inning as you sit

Hot dogs! Get Your Hot Dogs!

Suddenly you have a hankering for a hot dog

Yep that always works

Hot dogs! Get Your Hot Dogs!

A vendor is walking down the aisle parks the box

Flash him some green he presents a hot dog

Take it

Eat it

Mmmm good

Are we having fun yet?

By the way in this bit of minutiae

Perhaps by sense of smell or taste

Is it all starting to come back to you now?

Is memory working?

Justifying

Identifying

Reinforcing

No?

Then eat another hot dog

Three up and three down

Outfielder Tim Raines is tossing the ball

To the bullpen catcher between innings

The Indians have scored a run

That fourth hot dog was much better than the first three

Chicago street relish has that tangy zip

It's the ninth inning now Cleveland down by five

Here is the pitch

Struck him out

Ball game

The White Sox beat the Indians 6 to 1

Outside now the tuba player in the parking lot

Strikes up a victory rendition of Tequila

The happy patrons exit the lot rather quickly

Now back at the Corolla

Once named The Black Mariah

With vehicle tweaks as a tribute to Bud Cort

Now Mariah loves to guzzle 10W40

Great game

It is now September 1, 1991 5:35PM

Time to start the drive back to Baltimore

It is well over 750 miles so the drive will take all night

The condition of the vehicle

According to it's arrival a week earlier

Is a hesitancy to shut ignition off when hot

As a potential failure on restart is inevitable

...38 miles...

...83 miles... turn on the headlights...

...145 miles...

...202 miles...no stops in Indiana...

...287 miles...stop for gas in Ohio leave car running...

...323 miles...

...407 miles...you are somewhere in Pennsylvania...

...471 miles...on the Pennsylvania Turnpike...

...559 miles...get gas don't turn car off...

...611 miles...you've entered the great state of Maryland...

...685 miles...you are reaching the last 100 miles of your trip...

...its nearly 5AM...

Green

...733 miles...just minutes away from the first light of day...

The cassette deck plays

My Daydream by Smashing Pumpkins

Nearing the end of I-70

Green

Onto the Baltimore Beltway here we go

The dashboard clock reads 6:13 am

Back on Eastern Standard Time

Green

The sun rises

The dew on the hood of the car...

The cool autumn air keeping the car from overheating...

Green

The sweet smell of hysteria

The last Baltimore Beltway exit approaches

Everything has gone green

Green

Taking the exit to the townhouse off US-1

It's the first traffic signal in three states

Don't doze now you're almost home

It's Green

Green

Green

I said the light

Yeah its Green

Green

Did you know Two Thousand One was also Green

And The Arizona Diamondbacks won The World Series?

Johnson & Johnson

———

September 11, 2001 6:13 AM Baltimore Beltway I-695

Onto the Baltimore Beltway

...It is now 6:13 am...

...the sun rises...

...the dew on the hood of the car...

...the cool autumn air keeping the car from overheating...

...the sweet smell...hysteria...

...the exit Baltimore I-95 New York approaches...

Driving an 88 Honda Accord Green no AC no radio

Headed towards New York City

As a courier you need to stop along the way

In the town of New Brunswick, New Jersey

Visit the headquarters of Johnson & Johnson

Deliver a legal box

Itinerary check

Roll down the window

The air is so clean and perfect

The dawn sky is glorious an exciting trip beckons

A similar morning so long ago

A Déjà vu

Ten years gone by now

Ten Years

Humming along to a song in your head

Smashing Pumpkins My Daydream

Smashing Pumpkins My Daydream

The package on the passenger seat

Just a small brown legal box not too heavy

There is an address printed on it :

From: Venable, LLP

2 Hopkins Plaza

Baltimore, MD 21201

Please ship to:

Johnson & Johnson

One Johnson & Johnson Plaza

New Brunswick, NJ 08933

The drive goes something like this

Start at 2 HOPKINS PLZ, BALTO on BALTIMORE ST - go 2.5 mi

Take ramp onto I-895 NORTH toward NEW YORK - go 1.0 mi

Merge onto I-95 NORTH - go 58.8 mi

I-295 exit toward NEW JERSEY TRNPIKE/DEL MEM BR/NJ-NY -

Go 61.4 mi

Take ramp onto NEW JERSEY TPKE N toward

NEW YORK/NEWARK - go 16.2 mi

NEW JERSEY TPKE NORTH becomes I-95 NORTH - go 14.4 mi

Exit 9 onto RT-18 NORTH toward NEW BRUNSWICK - go 3.1 mi

Take ramp onto ALBANY ST[RT-27] toward PRINCETON - go 0.2 mi

Turn on JOHNSON AND JOHNSON PLZ - go 0.1 mi

Arrive at 1 JOHNSON AND JOHNSON PLZ, NEW BRUNSWICK

Here at the Johnson & Johnson Headquarters

It is September 11, 2001 at 9:05 AM

There is a security guard that directs you to a concierge desk

Where someone can sign for the package

He is an elderly gentleman in uniform seated behind a desk

Staring in shock at a TV console that is beside him

Handing the package to the concierge he accepts the delivery

Signs the manifest

With the work part of the drive over it is off to NYC for play time

Before that call the office in Baltimore

They will need confirmation of the delivery

Car dispatcher, please

One second...

...

Hey man, where are you?

... ...

I'm just leaving Johnson & Johnson delivered the package

What's up?

What do you mean what's up?

A plane just crashed into the World Trade Center!

... ...

Weird

... ...

Probably some sort of stunt or something

... ...

I dunno just hurry back

Cancel the rest of your trip

I need you back here

Lonnie Ximenez

As a young only child

Born October 12, 1934 in Metairie, Louisiana

Lonnie was quite talented on the piano

A musical distraction to his mothers failing health

A sad young boy in the bayou

With a frazzled ill-fitting suit for the funeral

He would see his childhood uprooted

His father Eliades took a job out of the air force

With Boeing and moved the pair to Seattle

Eliades would always point his son towards music

To be something anything that he couldn't be

So it was no great surprise that Lonnie

Who found schoolwork to be tedious

Found music to be his passion

By the time of high school

The schoolwork even more tedious and ignored

When the job kept his father away too long

Lonnie would hitch rides out of town

Chasing the Rocking Chair of Ray Charles

Stretching further out

Olympia Tacoma Renton

To check out all the music venues blues jazz

Of course he dug the great LP records

Mostly Louie

Dizzy

Minnie

As a young man now he realized that Seattle

Was not where he wanted to be

The action was in Chicago

Chi-town

Eliades Ximenez worked very hard at Boeing

And when he suddenly suffered and died of a heart attack

Lonnie would have to be on his own

Losing both parents certainly took its toll

But Eliades left him quite a lot of savings

His father was a good responsible man

Who saved the money to one day see his son

Go to and graduate college

No rumpled suit for this funeral

Lonnie would not go on to college

He would go to Chicago instead

He never made it big as a musician

He tried and tried

But something better

Much better

Would happen along the way

Her name was Dorothea Haywood

And it was she who turned Lonnie

Onto the Chicago music scene

Chess Records

Muddy Waters

Willie Dixon

Howlin' Wolf

Lonnie became close with Dorothea

She had family up north in Wisconsin

And with no family of his own

He wanted a family with her

And he got along with all of Dorothea's relatives

They would take frequent trips to Milwaukee

The family off to the ballpark to see The Braves play

Lonnie took to this new love of baseball

Her brother Bernard and Lonnie would

Hop the fences and try to sneak into the baseball games

For free

His favorite player was of course Hammering Hank

Hall Of Fame Milwaukee Brave Henry Aaron

Not long after Lonnie and Dorothea settled down

A small house on the North Side of Chicago

Dorothea was a loving wife with the big extended family

And soon they were expecting a child

Lonnie was over the moon

He deeply missed his father and wanted this child

He had become a middle school music teacher

Coached little league on the side

The kids teased him because he wasn't a Chicago Cubs fan

Nor the White Sox

During her pregnancy

Dorothea worked odd jobs odd hours

Cashier bank clerk typist as long as she could

But Lonnie wanted her to stay home while expecting

Dorothea had her secrets

She had a special gift that she spoke little to Lonnie about

She was clairvoyant

She studied Marquis de Puységur

The somnambulist and hypnotist

Visitors would stop by their home to have readings

She was known to practice mesmerism

She was planning to be a stay at home mom

Pretty soon the couple would be discussing names

What do you think Lon?

If it is a boy I want him to be named after Hank Aaron

So what do you think?

You and your baseball

If a girl Simone

Lon

Look I see something special in the future

Maybe it is our child just maybe

The name is Edson

He will be a great one Lon

One of the greatest classical guitarists of his era

I love you Doe

Just a few weeks later

Lonnie and Dorothea

Welcome their first and only child to the world

On July 23, 1957 in Chicago, Illinois

They name their newborn baby boy

Henri Edson Ximenez

Forsyth Park

———

Hey

Hey wake up

Uh huh on a park bench

A frisbee zinged by and clocked you in the forehead

Didn't have much affect

You were dozing off on a park bench

It is afternoon the weather is clear a bit humid

Check your watch

4:16 PM

Almost forgot

It's November 14, 1998

This is somewhere in the city of Savannah, Georgia

That's your knapsack which contains

An unwrapped hefty trash bag liner

A journal

Several cassette tapes

Oh this isn't any old park bench

No sir this is the spectacular Forsyth Park

It is Savannah's largest and most opulent

Strolling paths lined with graceful moss laden live oak trees

Scented magnolias azaleas and marigolds surround

One of the world's most beautiful fountains

The famous Forsyth Park Inn overlooks it all

A dozen dogs and their owners playfully chase frisbees

Grab the journal it's a relative newer one

A few photographs fall from it

Aha that's a polaroid taken in the master bedroom

The three windows to the south decorated with

Various hanging plants and flower pots on the window ledge

The two ficus trees on either side of a halfway-filled aquarium

On those ficus trees strands of Spanish moss hanging

Intermingling

Small clumps of moss laying in the dirt of the flower pot

Wrapped around each tree

There is also more moss attached to the hanging plants

It is in the windows which form privacy drapes

That extends all the way to the ground

The moss in these photos looks rather pale and withered

Is this gardening or scenery you tell me?

Put the photos back in the journal

Let's examine the frisbee that grazed your head

There is a great deal of dog slobber on it

A border collie looks your way patiently

Go for it

You toss he runs he leaps

Do they ever miss?

There is a small clump of Spanish moss on the ground

There are gobs and gobs of it all over the park

No sense taking it

What are you going to put it in?

Oh yes I did say something about a trash bag liner

How convenient

Yes those old bedroom photos had the dying lichen everywhere

Let's put two and two together

Don't laugh

Pick it up

It is a thirty gallon hefty trash bag

Roomy ample voluminous

It is black on the inside green on the outside

Standard issue

I mean if you're keeping track of that sort of thing

Pick up the piece of Spanish moss

I'm not kidding

Place it in the trash bag

To replace those withered bits back home

Decoration or art or foliage or whatever

It's your bag man literally

Now strolling through the park

Here we find a beautiful fountain in the middle

The Forsyth Park fountain is a large ornate two-tiered

Cast-iron fountain surmounted by a classically robed

Female figure standing in extreme contrapposto

Holding a rod

Water comes from this rod into the top basin

In which she is standing

Nearby a live oak with some moss dangling on a branch

Talk about low hanging fruit

Reach up and grab a hunk off the tree

At the end of the park an old mansion

The Mansion on Forsyth Park is chic and luxurious

Inspired by the artistic drama of historic exterior design

Contemporary interiors accentuated

With over 400 pieces of original artwork

A gourmet restaurant a tranquil spa

Hands-on cooking classes for an extraordinary

Cultural experience

In architecture art music and cuisine

It's all that and a bag of chips

To the front sugar magnolia and palm trees

Pretty amazing though not suitable for your budget

But hey

Even more Spanish moss

Where do they get it all?

Who puts it all over these trees?

No sense wasting any space in that bag

Pick up the pieces until you're full

Ok done

Now let's find the transportation

A year ago it would have been the truck

And when you exit the park to West Hall Street

Lo and behold

There she be

A few more dents and the incessant tick-tick-ticking

But better luck than I have with vehicles

It is almost like I'm jinxed with bad cars

A jinx or a h-

Never mind

Must be about oil changes

Toss the trash bag into the back

Onto the covered bed liner of the truck

No worries don't think anyone will steal it

Folks are nice down here in these parts

West Hall street is one of the four boundary streets of Forsyth Park

Time to clean up and dine across the street

At The Lucky Savannah Cafe

Hey!

Saturdays they have half-price frittatas

Nice a small table where you can relax kick back

It's now November 14, 1998 6:54 PM

Sitting comfortably by the front bay window

A calm mood enhanced by the afternoons exercise

Outside a gas lamp pops on in the dusk

Enjoy a chai latte

Get some caffeine in your wiring

It might be a good time to do some reading

Or writing or both

Let's check out that journal more closely

A glossy color print document stored in the inner sleeve

A remnant from a press kit entitled

New Orleans Bath

New Orleans Bath

PRESS RELEASE by Kevin Lundahl

It was the best and worst of times

So what happens if it was the most indifferent?

New Orleans Bath is a forty minute music video

Taking you along for the drive from

Baltimore to New Orleans

With stops along the way in Louisville and Memphis

The trip in autumn of 1997

Originally a spring trip was aborted

Planning Baltimore Savannah Tampa New Orleans

Unfortunately things went bad in Tampa

A 15 hour U-Turn canceled sights from The Big Easy

Check one in each column for best and worst of times

By the fall of 1997 plans were back on course

In the second week of November the voyage began

Before the voyage a recording commenced

At the Peabody Sound music room

A Casio Keyboard

An Ibanez Analog Delay

A Fender Super Reverb

Created lovely organ sounds that went to cassette

In wide dynamic two-track stereo

These snippets played a wonderfully creepy soundtrack

Forcing a slight change in itinerary

The vacation turned into a work assignment

A last minute grab for the Sony Camcorder

A script was hastily thrown together for filming

Throughout the trip down to Louisiana

The idea was to take full advantage of the camera filters

Solarize sepia black and white negative

Video recorded November 10-15, 1997

The soundtrack captures a blend of church organ

Calliope circus music new age piano

That embellishes the strangeness which is mostly out/in focus

Light and shadow fade to black

There are twenty tunes most under two minutes

The Baltimore footage starts on a Charles Village Rooftop

At dawn

And across the 29th street bridge as morning breaks

By the third tune we go from a solarized shot of a bridge

To a black and white shot of a cathedral in Louisville

Negative-transposed shots of blackbirds and power lines

Seem out of place in Memphis

Then before you know it The Big Easy

The rest of the video takes place there

With shots in the French Quarter

New Orleans Museum of Art

The Garden District at St. Charles

All playing a prominent theme

Balloons coffins antique cars Spanish moss

Are some of the images that give you the creeps

The Colonel Short cornstalk house

Along with extensive shots in St. Louis Cemetery #1

Apparently an over indulgence

In the Mardi Gras footage of Easy Rider

One clever technique is to include title screens

Where each tune is called a chapter

Corresponding to a maxim or colloquialism

Helping the viewer understand it all with added emphasis

The author claims the trip to be one of the most

Indifferent

Adventures he has undertaken

The voyeur indeed

Showing the cameraman to be shy

Obvious in crowds almost nervously

Turning away expecting transparency

A calming slow deliberate pace and panning

Which echoes the slow syrupy reverberant drone

Of the keyboard sound

Nothing really exciting ever happens

Then again no misfortune befalls the hero

It seems only fitting since all the good and bad melodrama

Was already played out of the system

Earlier in the year

Good news for all of us

-K. L.

Cyanosis

———

Henri Edson Ximenez was born at St. Luke's Hospital in Chicago

It was considered the top children's hospital

In all of Cook County

There was a slight problem with Henri

He arrived with blue baby syndrome

It is a condition often referred to as Cyanosis

Which is the blueness of the skin in babies

As a result of low oxygen levels in the blood

The treatment in the 1950-60s was to keep the baby warm

Place the baby in an incubator

He looks a little blue Doe

The doctor said it is short term and he will be fine

I don't know Lon

This is not right this is not what I saw

What I felt

As he was growing inside me

I have a bad feeling about this

About our little baby boy

During the initial diagnosis the infant may fail to thrive

Be lethargic

It can be complicated with lung problems

Such as nasal flaring and possible seizures

A rapid heartbeat and respiratory rate

A shortness of breath

While Dorothea was pessimistic

Lonnie paid extra attention to the doctor's prognosis

While it can be considered postpartum depression

Dorothea was empty inside

Depression

She had already opened the door into the world

Of Franz Mesmer

Her beliefs in mesmerism contributed to

Losing attention with her child

Henri would be fine

He grew up with a slight build but was still very playful

And Lonnie wasted no time teaching him to play baseball

Against all odds

Lonnie didn't play baseball himself of course

As a child

His father Eliades was the one

Who pushed him towards the piano

Trying to be something anything that he couldn't be

As a little league coach

Lonnie saw this irony

The first year in baseball was trying

They put Henri in right field

All the boys batted and threw right-handed

So seldom was there ever a ball hit to his side of the field

All the boys who registered for the team got to play

There were a dozen kids and Lonnie was the manager

The uniforms arrived and the parents were given numbers

To sew onto their kids jersey

Lonnie asked the kids to pick their number between one and twelve

When he asked Henri the response was

43

Because Henri liked to watch Richard Petty race his stock car

On the ABC Wide World of Sports on Saturday afternoons

And 43 was the number painted on the Blue and Red Plymouth

No son pick one through twelve

In his first at bat

He took the first two pitches for balls

And then he took the next three pitches for strikes

He didn't swing his bat at all in that first game

Dad I didn't think any of those pitches were strikes

In the following games he started to swing

But all he hit was air and struck out for the whole season

Then in the last game

He swung and connected

The ball hit the ground and rolled down to the third baseman

Henri just stood there frozen

With a big smile on his face

I connected

The third baseman picked up the ball

And was confused to see Henri just standing in the batters box

The teammates screamed to Henri run down to first base run

He dropped the bat and started running

Got thrown out by six steps

When he returned to the bench

Lonnie the manager

And also Lonnie the father

Asked one question

Why didn't you run son?

Dad

There will be plenty of times when I'll be doing just that

Unison Velvatone

———

Another cup of chai latte at Lucky Savannah's

The previous set of journal pages were in pristine condition

Compared to the haphazard state of the rest

There is a similar press release like the one

Kevin Lundahl wrote on New Orleans Bath

Seems like the top portion of the article is missing

We can pick up in mid sentence after the torn bits

And it goes like this :

..- ...- ...——... ...—of the recordings done in 1994

were passed on to Tony and Adam. The three gentleman constituted a band

performing selected songs under various band names including Blinder and Silt Flats

They recorded a session in the fall of 1994 at Social Services Recording Studio

"I Want You" was chosen for this collection the rest of the session has been lost

This lineup also cooked up some goodies in early 95 recorded at The Hour Haus

"The Brown Scarf", "Wire Song", "The Victrola Idler", "Buffaloes", "Stumbelin",

"Culvert Gardenia", "Astronaut Satellite", all eventually touched up at

Social Services Recording Studio in the Spring of 1995

There was one more solo project that spring

at The Hour Haus from that came "Super Thin Alien" and "Honest"

Two more noteworthy events happened that spring: "Helikopter" reunited

and that lineup of Unison Velvatone ceased

"Ride across Oklahoma" was recorded at 824 Park Ave

It would later be performed in 1996 by the next lineup of which included Colin

"Dirt Roads" has special significance

It predicts the demise of the Unison Velvatone lineup

This was a band with vision and spark

who often got derailed through the many personnel changes

and extraneous band compromises over

three tumultuous years

LISTEN TO THE TAPES AND GET BACK TO ME,

- Colin

———————

OK superstar

Let me help you out a bit here

This passage leads to evidence of a musical career

It includes people you have assembled bands with

A bunch of songs I have heard

Though

Hardly any other earthly presence anywhere else has

One of the bigger nuggets mentions the band name

Unison Velvatone

And also that it has ceased being a band

That second word Velvatone is not misspelled

It refers to a spiral bound notebook manufacturer

From the 1960s

And you found one of those in your attic summer 1992

A green notebook containing a diary song lyrics and tabs

No evidence of who wrote it mostly in pencil

The book was passed about by the Helikopter band members

For their amusement only

No songs were stolen

The best thing about the notebook

Was giving the future group it's name

The second biggest nugget indicates page notes

By a person named Colin

You remember

He was one of your roommates

The one who digs motorcycles

So the conclusion is that there are tapes to find

Listen to

And continue to evolve the music within

Make it last make it endure

As a fragment of your life

That you cannot do without

That you know no other way

As Rainer Maria Rilke

Suggested in his Letters To A Young Poet

Let's keep digging in that journal

It is probably the most tangible device we have

To keep that memory strong and current

Up to date

Relevant

Whatever wherever that is

The third part of the journal has a printout

Of what looks like a primitive web page

Perhaps constructed by a novice using HTML

It doesn't have the same snap and sparkle of those

Kevin Lundahl press releases

Maybe it is under construction

Let's take a peek :

Main Street Physics

Felt good to twist

Felt good to turn

It felt so good

Laying there

And we are all

Alone

I felt u breathe

I felt u squirm

I fell apart

Understand

U were there

Laying under me

I saw us on a bridge

A Japanese Footbridge

Turning softly

On your soul

Whispering in

I felt those needs

The needs to control things

Grabbing firmly

On yr dress

And yr response

Was clinging on to me

early UNIFORM history

The Original Lineup of UNIFORM was Colin (drums), Christian (guitar), and _____ (Bass and Vocals)

The first live show was in July 1997 at a warehouse located

at 921 E. Fort Ave in Baltimore, MD

"Main Street Physics", "Hostage Of Luck",

"Heavenly Hopeful", "Destination: Stars and Stripes",

and "Row-houses of the Holy"

were some of the songs performed at that show

Most of those songs were recorded

at Mount Royal Recording Studio by Charley in December of 1997

original T-shirt design - Colin 1997

Clever way to get Monet in a tune

What Main Street Physics means is a riddle

The titles are intriguing I give you that

Also from this bit the name Uniform pops up

The name Christian appears in this entry

You are a collaborator that's good

Let's jot that stuff down and move on

It is November 14, 1998 10:21PM

After writing in your journal and doing some reading

Enjoying your chai latte it is time to roll out

Maybe even go for a drive

The frittata?

Well

OK at best?

Hey

What do you want for half price

Believe And Want

———

Henri went hitless his first year in little league

Things began to change in year two

Now a year older than the new arrival pee wee kids

He played more positions and most importantly

Pitcher and Catcher

He preferred catcher the most he liked talking to everyone

The plate umpire opposing hitters parents

Though he may not have possessed athletic gifts

He still retained the gift of gab

Lonnie was still managing the team

Maybe it was the stress of the marriage

Job

Child

Little League coach

Lonnie just couldn't cut back on his Marlboro cigarettes

Two three packs a day

His brother in law Bernard would come to Chicago

To watch his nephew's games and also visit his sister

Dorothea spoke privately with Bernard

She didn't attend any of the baseball games

The relationship with Henri

Mother and son

Was strange and awkward to say the least

She believed being a mother was not God's plan for her

She mistakenly thought giving Lonnie a son was her duty

To replace the loss of his father Eliades

She grew to resent Henri

And was upset that Lonnie was more reticent inhibited distant to her

And closer to their son

Bernard would be her consultant and confidant

I believe in the existence within myself of a power

She would tell Bernard

Directly quoting from Marquis de Puységur

The entire doctrine of Believe And Want

I Believe that I have the power to set into action

The Vital Principle of Man

I Want to make use of it

This is all my science and all my means

From this belief derives my will to exert it

Don't you see Bernard

Believe And Want

Bernard believed in his sister

And wanted her to find her path

Her practice in the study of Animal Magnetism

Led to many visitors at the small house on the North Side

Henri didn't understand it

Lonnie would take Henri to the backyard to play catch

He didn't want himself or Henri to witness these visits

What Dorothea believed was an ability

A power

To manipulate the magnetic fluid within each of her subjects

British magnetizers distanced themselves from this variation

Of Mesmerism

Dorothea channeled what her clients thought

Was a magnetic fluid in the brain

This was done physically by a process known as

The laying on of hands

Lonnie and Dorothea now engaged in bitter arguments

This family of three was struggling

Trying to pay off the house

The smoking and now the drinking

Would take its toll on Lonnie Ximenez

Bernard was in-between the marital strife

He got along very well with Henri a loving uncle

Told him stories of sneaking into Braves games to watch

Henry Aaron play that's Henry with a Y

Bernard was always around now

And he would help Lonnie coach little league

One day

The kids showed up for the game

The manager did not

Bernard called the school and something happened to Lonnie

He suffered a massive heart attack

He did not survive

The same tragic end like his father Eliades Ximenez

Would split the family apart

After the funeral

Dorothea was completely incoherent disturbed irrational

She could not and would not be mentally or physically capable

Of raising Henri

With tears on his cheek Bernard had to make a painful decision

One he would fully never come to terms with

To have his sister committed

The affairs of the Ximenez family in Chicago were closed

Bernard would raise Henri

He needed a job and a fresh start and called around

He got a return call from Cliff a friend from high school

Hey man

I moved to Tennessee and they are hiring down at the power company

Oh yeah?

Yeah

I'll call down there for you

Put in a good word

Thanks man

And it all worked out

Henri and Bernard were moving to Tennessee

The promise of a new frontier and a new future

Like Voight to New York then with Ratso to Florida

While the new job taking care of them was at

Memphis Light Gas & Water

UV-373

Savannah

Midnight in the gas station with tapes and a truck

From your knapsack a handful of those cassette tapes

They all have UV-373 written on them

Plus a bunch of different three digit code numbers

A sheet of loose leaf wrapped around the tapes with rubber band

It serves as a table of contents or index of some sort

The page has matching three digit numbers

Let's hash the codes of the UV-373 Tapes :

> *101 ...the last time I was a teenager you told us...*
>
> *Colin and I invented this in the drum salon prior to Montana*
>
> *The background scratching from the Kraftwerk Computer World LP*
>
> *Played backwards with the Fostex four track into the Fender Super Six*
>
> *Recorded with AKAI condenser mikes on Colin's reel to reel*
>
> *104-105 Astrophysics*
>
> *A*
>
> *B*
>
> *Melissa the punished child in the stolen makeup*
>
> *As in Already Dead by Denis Johnson*

The next Hitchcock girl

114- Burning Charisma - redo alternate verses throughout

119- conga tune - the new city ceramic-brick-ceramic

121-122-123 Culvert Gardenia

124 - Da Do Da Do

125 - escalator/power/mechanical blackbirds in Memphis?

203 - Ghost girl in the desert

Hard to reproduce distortion effect on guitar

219 - song 9-73 recording clips meters nicely but

225 - de es-SSSS-er eliminate drum track or

possibly do over if unorthodox timing overlap is not figured out

reexamine bass/guitar keys

310 - Warminster

13

"She laughed as she stole her name from a summers night

With ruby lips she kisses circles in the sky

Her secrets kept in boxes locked with little lies

She could write an epic poem from a sleepy sigh"

"A fistful of daisy breeze full of marigold"

2 she could...she said so...said so...

...loop add drums at end...

Add to liner notes ->

"UV-373 constructed a rehearsal space

in 1995-96 known as the UV-373 drum salon"

So we see that song lyrics images structure

Are in a TBD condition

Raw

Untapped

Which inspired that idea in the journal

To take another listen and make improvements

That's great

Now let's get some gas and go

Are you feeling remarkably awake?

As if you could drive all night with the stereo cranked?

Let's start the truck and head towards Baltimore

Which is 620 miles away

On interstate 95 heading north pop in a tape

...21 miles...

...38 miles...

Too quiet and time to pick up the pace

Why not pop in another one of those tapes?

...87 miles...

"She laughs as she stole her name from a summers night"

...116 miles...

...177 miles...

"With ruby lips she kisses circles in the sky"

...217 miles...

...285 miles...

...316 miles...

"Her secrets kept in boxes locked with little lies"

...357 miles...

...414 miles....

...454 miles...

...503 miles...

"She could write an epic poem from a sleepy sigh"

...557 miles....

...596 miles...

"A fistful of daisy...a breeze full of marigold"

"Marigold..."

...617 miles

There you made it

Baltimore

Yes you still live on the corner of 30th and Calvert Streets

And got a lucky parking spot right in front of the apartment building

After listening all through the night to those tapes

Coming up with many new ideas of how to

Create edit and rework the magic in the music

In the bed liner of your truck is the luggage souvenirs

Plus the bag full of Spanish moss and other plant life

That you plan on using in decorating your bedroom

First you need to bolt upstairs for the bathroom

The jangling house keys are clumsily thrust into

The third floor apartment deadbolt

It is 9:12 AM Sunday morning

The rest of the building tenants are sleeping in

Enjoying a lazy Indian summer morning

As you weary from driving

Struggle to open the lock

Slamming the front door run for the bathroom

A few loose hardwood floor planks trigger

An empty Virgin Mary candle to rattle on the fireplace mantle

Next to a small piece of cemetery marble rubble AKA The Brick

As you toss your coat on the couch

And now that you have taken care of the paperwork

It is time to go back to the truck

And unload everything from your trip

Mortal Arthur

The jangling house keys are clumsily thrust into

The third floor apartment deadbolt

As you weary from driving

Struggle to open the lock

Slamming the front door run for the bathroom

A few loose hardwood floor planks trigger

An empty Virgin Mary candle to rattle on the fireplace mantle

Next to a small piece of cemetery marble rubble AKA The Brick

As you toss your coat on the couch

And now that you have taken care of the paperwork

You head back to the living room

Grab the remote control and turn on the TV

The somber news anchorperson revisits earlier footage

Of a crumbling World Trade Center tower

And then another tower

It is September 11, 2001 12:14 PM

And then the phone rings

Immediately recognizing the voice of Mortal Arthur

Hey are you watching this?

Just got in the door are you in Iceland?

I am but not for much longer

If not in Iceland then where?

Thinking about Quebec City

Bush is really fucked this time

When are you coming back?

I'm afraid that I am not coming back

I see

Well

I will miss you reading my Tarot

Well you could always return to New Orleans

Don't remind me what a phony

I'll call you again someday

Until then be well

I'm glad you posted our correspondences

Only on my site no one will see them

N3794N and the Arch Of Stone

Be careful in America

I will try take care of yourself

Click

You do realize that you'll never hear from him again?

Just then the phone rings a second time

Still distracted by the first call

With Mortal Arthur

And hypnotized by sad images on the television

Let the answering machine pick this one up

And a third call second message

Later on collect yourself check the machine

The Red light flashes twice

These are the two messages :

Beep :

"Hey It's Kevin,

Just wanted to let you know that we've shipped the new "Uniform" single

We decided on "Dictionary of Deconstructionists" for the A-Side

and "AP Hill Came to Dub" as the B-Side

There are test pressings here at the label stop by

Also the LP "Black And Vain" will be in stores by the end of the week

Congratulations I'll talk to you later"

Wow

All things considered

Be happy you stopped in New Brunswick today

Before continuing to New York

The music doesn't seem so important right now

Go ahead cancel the DC New York Boston tour dates

Hit the button for the second message

Beep Beep :

"Good evening sir

This is the Red Lion Hotel wake up call service

We are just calling to see if you would like

another 6:00 AM wakeup call for tomorrow

Please let us know so that we can

accommodate you properly

We hope you are enjoying your stay

here in the Emerald City

and we will see you tomorrow at check out

Thank You"!

©1991 Red Lion

After checking your two messages you notice something odd

The Red message light still flashes

Did you know Nineteen Ninety-One was also Red and

The Minnesota Twins won The World Series?

We'll cancel the TV screen

Ponder the first message

And dive into the second one

Let's flip back a decade

The Red Lion Hotel

Very accommodating for the business traveler

A king size bed with three plush pillows

A lovely view of the courtyard and swimming pool

All in its glory and splendor

It is August 28, 1991 7:15 PM

This is the Sea-Tac (Seattle & Tacoma) Red Lion Hotel

A wakeup phone call confirmed with the clerk

A small journal

Different then the one we perused

Is laying out

Don't ask me why

Maybe you lost one or two along the way

On the bathroom floor are soggy clothes

The ones worn at the Lollapalooza Festival

There is a mangled denim jacket

Concert snacks leftovers

Unrecognizably smashed into any and all of its pockets

A used capri-sun juice pouch where the straw

Is mangled and resembles a scorpions tail

A bag of granola raisins apple mushed

That would make good pie if prepared properly

Or sequentially

Remnants of a Chunky Bar if extracted from a cadaver's throat

(More on that later much later)

Or simply been in a mosh pit for too long

Over on the bed next to the journal

A Concert T-Shirt in decent shape

Stuffed down the pants pre concert

To prevent damage nice move

The Seattle Lollapalooza Concert T-Shirt lists

Jane's Addiction

Fishbone

Violent Femmes

Ice-T

Butthole Surfers

Siouxie And The Banshees

It fits you well will make good sleepwear

The journal mentions something about

Norwood Fisher and Brian Ritchie

Backstage handling each others bass

Electric and acoustic with mutual admiration

The journal also says something about

Leaving the concert early

Too much rain and mosh pit injuries

Oh well

Can't win em all champ

Tomorrow it's an early train

Fifty Two hours back to Chicago

One king-size bed yellow rose petal pattern comforter

It looks extremely inviting

zzzz...zzz ... zz....

zzzz...zzz ... zz....

yellow

zzz.... zzz... zzzz......

zzz.... zzz... zzzz......

yellow rose pattern

zzzz ...zzzz .... zzzz...

yellow

zzzz ...zzzz .... zzzz...

zzzz ...zzzz .... zzzz...

Any extended dream fall could send you traveling

You should be used to it by now but here goes

Did you know Nineteen Ninety-Eight was also Yellow

And The New York Yankees won The World Series?

Vinny

———

zzzz ...zzzz .... zzzz...

You were napping on your black leather sofa

The southern exposed windows to your left

Reveal a sunny November afternoon in Baltimore

It is the old bright apartment plaster and hardwood

A non-working fireplace straight ahead

On the mantel assorted knick-knacks including

A Virgin Mary votive candle

A snow globe

A broken motorcycle piston

Assorted rusted iron fittings gaskets washers

A 6-inch piece of cemetery marble rubble (known as The Brick)

A dried rose

To the right of the mantel there is a plush chair

Above it on the wall is a poster from The Silence of The Lambs

On the other side of the mantel is another plush chair

On the wall above it is a Led Zeppelin tapestry

A coat was tossed on the floor

There is a hefty bag full of Spanish moss in front of you

It is November 15, 1998 1:06 PM

To the right is an iguana cage

There is an iguana sleeping in the cage

Resting his head on an unpainted plaster gargoyle statue

The iguana cage is actually a 75 gallon aquarium

With a handmade screen placed on top

Extended all the way up almost to the ceiling

There is a ficus tree inside the tank

And the iguana has plenty of space to climb

And jump

And have a generally good time

A small bowl of water heat rock statue

Pea pebbles bark mulch line the bottom

The iguana has a name and it is Vinny Green Balls

So the local football team has a Vinny playing quarterback

And his last name is Testeverde

So it seemed like an obvious choice

Listen sounds like dishes clinking and running water

In the kitchen you greet Colin

Dude you were out - back from Savannah I see

Man how long was I out?

Not sure I see you have more Spanish moss

More Spanish moss but no cemetery bricks

How was the trip and the truck running?

Ran great went over 250000 miles I drove all night

The music kept me awake those tapes

Did you listen to all of them?

Of course

I'm going to master them into a UV-373 record

A band practice greatest hits as it were

You want to help with the editing?

Sure that's why I sent the note along

Though greatest hits records are for

Housewives and teenagers

Yeah I believe Bruce McCulloch used that line

Yeah whatever man

Oh I think your iguana is sick

???

Indeed the reptile looks rather pale

He is resting his head on the plaster gargoyle statue

Open the crisper in the refrigerator

Grab a few leaves of romaine lettuce

He likes spinach leaves also

There

Vinny responds by munching on a few salad greens

His color returns and he scampers around the cage

Touching the inside of the aquarium something is wrong

As the cage isn't as warm as usual

Surprised the iguana didn't turn blue

Like blue baby syndrome

So move the cold gargoyle statue to reveal the problem

Ah the blue heat rock beneath it

Looks like it has come unplugged

It is simply a rock attached to an AC power cord

Inspecting closely it has a frayed edge

Must have come unplugged while

Vinny was playing darting frolicking about

So grab the blue heat rock

Baby Blue

Pale Blue

Temporarily Non-Functioning Blue

Heat rock

And try to plug it bac-kkk-ZZZZZZZ-aaaa

                    ZAPPPPPPPPPP!!!!!!

I mentioned something earlier about

Don't touch batteries to your tongue

Yeah well

That is DC current easy stuff

This well it's 120 AC and it can kill you friend

You gave me no choice

Did you know Two Thousand Two was also Blue

And The California Angels won The World Series?

Blue seems new

911 Revisited

There is a knock on the door

Laurie the next door neighbor with a concerned look

I heard a loud thump did you fall down?

I'm not sure what happened

Do you need any help?

I was heading downstairs to the truck

I'll walk down with you

Thanks

No problem

I thought you had a car not a truck

Outside now Laurie sees you're OK and heads back in

It is dark the crisp air clears the cobwebs

Oh by the way

It is September 11, 2002 9:05 PM

No truck here it's the Honda Accord

Feeling thirsty?

Yeah when in doubt that's the way to figure it out

With it the One Year Anniversary of the 9-1-1 disaster

Maybe you will get your drunk on with friends

It's a hop in the Honda ten minutes to

Daugherty's Irish Pub

A parking spot on West Chase Street

Very close to the Meyerhoff Symphony Hall

And across the street from the Rite Aid pharmacy

You know just in case

It is a pleasant enough Irish pub

Decent food grog tables booths pool darts

The Irishman keeps the mix tape blaring in the dining room

A dimly lit establishment located in charming Mt Vernon

A long mirrored bar to the left with a copper-ish hue

There is a TV on showing some sporting event

The bar counter has a shiny copper texture to it

Reflected in the mirror that explains it

Tonight a few patrons minding their own drinks

And a handful of vacant barstools

And here he is Derrick the Irishman

What will ya have tonite lad?

Jim Beam and ginger ale

Switched off of the Guinness are we?

Ummm something lighter than liquid bread tonight yeah D

A fine choice lad

And a tab please don't want to bother your soccer game

They're also called a high ball so start slow

I get the feeling this could be a long night

Don't you get that same feeling?

With no acquaintances present you mosey on back

To the pool room two green felt tables often crowded

There is a jukebox in the corner belching out

Morphine's Cure For Pain

Oh and there's Sam the local pool hustler

You playing tonight?

Ah sure maybe sure

Put your name up on the chalkboard

Many many too many names on the chalkboard

Alex Brian Marc Terri Shelby Rachel Stumpy Joe Bill Just Bill

So it might be a while

A brief sway to the tone

Of distorted two string bass and sax drone

Where is the cave

Where the wise woman went?

And tell me where

Where's all that money that I spent?

Then a saunter back to the copper-tone bar

You about ready for another?

Oh you can bet your green un-dies I am!

You got it mate

Fabulous another Jim and Ginger

Things start looking up

In walks the excuse for this visit

Someone not quite walking onto a yacht

Though her perfume could smell

Like apricot

She's a writer

The one that you clip out articles of

We're talking about

The one and only

Ilsa Navas

This Thing

———

Sloshing through another Jim and Ginger are we

As she makes her way in

Like she normally would on a Wednesday evening

Hump day/night

And of course you just can't forget

This Thing

That you have for Ilsa Navas

Well if it isn't my favorite Scorpio!

Hello Ilsa yeah hey yeah that's you my favorite Scorpio too

Yes have you thought of a plan for our birthday?

Ummm something similar to this plan

As you raise your glass

Ilsa has been freelancing in the City Journal several years now

She did a deep dive into tower three

She investigated the money trail in the Angelos asbestos cases

And she has contributed to her passion in the arts

With reviews of up and coming local bands

Including yours

So what's the word in the art scene?

Raissa they call her the chicken lady

A new exhibit going up in October

That I'm really excited about

The chicken lady?

You mean like on The Kids In The Hall?

Hah no no she is a painter

She uses imagery of the chicken as a central motif

Sort of as an icon connected to faith

Very Catholic

At least from the bit I have seen

Imagistic impressionistic cinema verite perhaps

Her paintings inform and have a great reverence

For traditional mediums

Hmmm

Back in a sec

As her musky perfume drifts away

The attention shifts to Derrick coming over

The scoreless soccer game goes to the thrilling extra time

How are you doing lad?

I guesssssss I could deal with anotherrrrrr

Coming right up mate

Swweeeee-ttt

Yet another Jim and Ginger

So much for .08

Strategizing Ilsa would not be easy

More so in the condition your condition was in

Adversaries of that scent were trolling nearby

The musky perfume returns with a giggle

I'm back sorry to be rude I saw an old friend

So how are you? Where have you been?

Not in the dirty south I can tell you that

I'm back from some lame shows in New York City

911 means something else altogether to me

Yeah I expect the usual suspects to file in and mope

It's been one year since my band released the record

Really! It came out on that same day?

Yup

Exactly and we never really celebrated it

I know The Uniform right? What was the song called again?

Dictionary of Deconstructionists

That's right DOD so why are you bummed?

The music business has been rather dull

Rather lousy rather uninspiring while the nation

Well while the nation

Is in conflict with Sad'm and the Eye-rackies

Bin Laden you mean

That's what I said right

Right and the Afghan Whigs

Do you think its just the music business or is there more to it?

I'm starting to think I'm jinxed or have a uh a HEX

REALLY? That's interesting...

Hmmm hold on for a sec

In a continual display of bad timing we see

Sam the pool hustler step up

Stick still in hand he never puts it down

Hey man you're up

Ummm skip my turn this time Sam

Whatever dude I have other victims waiting

Right

Go slay em Minnesota

Fortunately Ilsa did not disappear again

Call it the Jim Beam but opportunity presents itself

Her curly black hair and deep brown eyes speak up

Mercury is in retrograde that could be it

But why a HEX?

I got a brick out of a cemetery about five years ago

What? Where did you get it?

I picked it up off a grave in New Orleans

And then you hear that laughing snort

Her endearing nasal vapor lock

That you find so completely irresistible

With a dimpled smile and squinty eyes she continues

You gotta take that brick back!

Take it back, why?

You desecrated a burial site

The Evil Spirits are pissed

Am I supposed to believe that?

It's your life it's your luck

So much for the imminent move Romeo

Things have decompressed

It is now time to parry

The plan didn't work it is time for a new one

Yeah well

Whatever well uh

I gotta use the John I'll be right back

A short wobble to the bathroom dialing up the sink

A splash of cold water on the face in retreat

Hoping to regroup rather quickly before

The Red Bulls swoop in on your Ilsa

This Thing

That you have for Ilsa Navas

Drunk skittish and now thinking too much

About that damn brick

The Evil Spirits are pissed?

What the Fu-

The cool water cannot quite pull your wits back

Starting to sober up but not quite enough to drive

Here look up notice the Orange stucco paint?

That Orange from the Wayside T-shirt Stand?

That Orange from behind Jan's bathrobe?

That Orange juice knocked over at the gargoyle shop?

Also for an Irish pub

This is an awfully small bathroom

It looks more like a motel sized bathroom

Uh-oh

Did you know Nineteen Ninety-Seven was also Orange

And The Florida Marlins won The World Series?

Well obviously

More importantly

Historians will note this as a smart ruse

To negate the DUI

The Saint Charles Motel

———

Let's say affordability is high on the list

Of this New Orleans motel rooms assets

Just a full size bed table chair bathroom

Unplugged mini fridge

It is November 13, 1997 8:55 PM

Here we are room 113 at the Saint Charles Motel

The camcorder walkman both recharging

The typewriter on the table

What little clothes you brought are at the foot of the bed

Open up the front door of this quaint temporary abode

Let some swampy humid miry air not unclear the head no sir

There is a sheet in the typewriter carriage

Half full here is a peek :

November 13, 1997

8:55 AM

NOMA - got there a little early... more on that later...

10:57 AM

Didn't stay long in the garden district...but I did ride a street car...

12:03 PM

I decided another day in the French Quarter for more recording...

1:15 PM

I walked down Bourbon Street...entered a saloon...started filming...

the bartender didn't care...fine...

I recorded more black/white footage for the creepy organ song

"Death of a Country Singer"...

2:05 PM

Immediately outside I saw three consecutive horse-drawn carriages...

parading down Bourbon Street...switched the lens to sepia...pressed record...

made the video for the song "Happy Loving Couples"...

4:16 PM

Very pleased with the days shoot...caught sunset at NOMA...

The New Orleans Museum of Art...where earlier in the day

I did the museum tour and the Fabergé egg collection on exhibit...

Now I point the camera to the geese flying low...

Landing on the courtyard reflecting pool...

This twilight became the music video "Motivational Afternoon"...

only a couple more songs and this film will wrap...

5:13 PM

I've started picking up pieces of Spanish moss along the way...

I toss it in the back of the truck...

It will look great in the bedroom...

Covering the trees and the hanging plants...

And add privacy to the curtain-less windows...

Good night

zzzz...zzzz...zzz...

zzzz...zzzz...zzz...

zzzz...zzzz...zzz...

z!

Base Hit

———

zzzz...zzzz...zzz...

"The pitch to David Ortiz..."

zzz.... zzz...z zzz...

"...he swings and a line drive BASE HIT over second base!"

zzz.. zzz.. hmm zzz...

"...here comes Johnny Damon rounding third!"

"...he's gonna SCORE!!!!!"

"RED SOX WIN THE GAME, 5 to 4 !!!!"

zzzzzz......zzzzz......what...

zzzzzz......zzzzz......what...

It is October 18, 2004 10:20PM

At the Mt Vernon apartment in downtown Baltimore

On the TV set a baseball game has just ended

You missed it

Like a bored security agent asleep at the console

I can give you the recap

The Boston Red Sox are jumping all over each other

As they have just defeated The New York Yankees 5-4

In Game Five of the 2004 American League Championship Series

As a huge Yankees fan the images

On the TV will certainly create a fantastically bad mood

The Red Sox jubilantly celebrating

It can make one sick in the stomach

Base Hit

By the looks of things the television

Should be shut off

They will have to win it in the Bronx now

Look over to the window sill ledge facing west

There lies the brick from Saint Louis Cemetery #1

The Brick

The Brick is mocking you!

At least you aren't as unlucky as The Red Sox

They are the ones with the HEX

Or rather

The Curse of The Bambino

The clouds suddenly release and the sill is pelted by raindrops

Another unusually warm mid-October Baltimore thunderstorm

Also on the window sill is a tiny tribute

To Rodan

A 3-D puzzle of The Kiss

Augustus Rodan's birthday is November 12

The same for Neil Young and Charlie Manson

The computer beeps

Indicating that an online chat window closed :

> *10/18/2004 10:02:33 PM Octoberiffic you You there?*
>
> *10/18/2004 10:02:56 PM Octoberiffic you Did you fall asleep*
>
> *watching the game?*
>
> *10/18/2004 10:03:08 PM Octoberiffic you ...*
>
> *10/18/2004 10:04:28 PM Octoberiffic !!!*
>
> *(signout)*

Before you can reply

Octoberiffic has signed off for the night

Outside the neighbors security light comes on in the alley

Looking out at the rain

A spider web strewn with rain pellets

A missing spider

After this unfortunate turn of events it's time

To venture out in the rain for some comfort food

Downstairs we go having visions of

A Chorizo chimi-changa with refried beans

Twice fried for extra crispiness

On the street you spot a white 1992 Toyota Camry

Yup unfortunately that's your new whip

A hardly suitable replacement for the stylish Accord

That Honda had a terminal transmission issue

Already miss the pop up headlights

It is October 18, 2004 11:03 PM

This rig is not a good cold starting one

Nor reliable

Nor a handling in the rain kind of vehicle

Still it is off to Holy Frijoles for Mexican food

A fine restaurant located in the Baltimore community of Hamden

Fire it up and the drive will go like this :

1. Start at 800 N CHARgggggggghhhhhLES ST, BALTIMORE

Going toward READ ST -

WHOA BUDDY Bear onto I-83 NfffffffffffkkkkkkkkkkkkkkkORTH -

Go 1.4 mi

3. Take exidddddddddt 8/MD-vvvvvvvvvv25 NORTH onto

FALLS RD[MD-25] - go

4. Turn on WdgjkT - go 0.2 mi

Arrive at 908 W 36TH ST, BALddddddORE, on the

WHOA BUDDY

OOPS!

DRIVING COMPUTER

FATAL ERROR

A Green Plymouth Duster cut you off

Green

Did you know Two Thousand One was also Green

And The Arizona Diamondbacks won The World Series?

You couldn't stand that Camry anyway

Did A Plane Really Crash?

After the DRIVING COMPUTER malfunction

Back in the drivers seat with another vehicle

Not the Nissan Truck nope

Not the Toyota Corolla

Yes it's the beloved Honda Accord

With those very same pop up headlights

It is September 11, 2001 10:15 AM

Driving south on Interstate 95

Just outside of New Brunswick, New Jersey

There is a message on the traffic alert sign

Issuing this unsettling warning

ALL ROADS INTO NEW YORK CITY ARE CLOSED

Continue southbound though very concerned

And now getting closer to

The Philadelphia International Airport

Crossing from New Jersey into Pennsylvania

As the airport approaches be on the lookout

For another traffic alert sign that reads

AIRPORT IS CLOSED THERE ARE NO FLIGHTS

Are you getting a little more anxious and disturbed?

I certainly would be

Why don't you turn on the radio?

Try and find out what is really going on

Oh that's right someone broke into the car

Months ago

Stole it

How good is the reception on that cell phone?

Yeah the cell phone spotty at best

Magic Messengers dispatch

This is Sally how can I help you

Hey it's me what's going on?

WHERE THE HELL ARE YOU?

I'm near the Philly Airport and it's closed

Did A Plane Really Crash?

Into the World Trade Center?

Or was Gary just pulling my leg?

GET YOUR ASS BACK HERE!

Since your last call a plane crashed into The Pentagon and

Oh shit

We have drivers heading to DC and back

And another plane crashed

I'll get back as fast as I can

Hang up and press on the gas pedal

As you speed up aren't you concerned that

You might get a speeding ticket?

But wait

There aren't any cops on the road

Hardly any cars

OK gun the engine to 90 miles per hour

Hold on hold on wait a second wait

Forget thinking about getting a ticket

What if you swerve off the road?

There is NO ONE on the road to help you out!

All police fire ambulance elsewhere

So slow your ass back down

To 55 miles per hour

Better rethink this one Jazzbo

Better rethink it quick

About ninety minutes later

Back on 30th street at the apartment

Anxious to get inside and flip on the television

See what really happened on the news

Hastily climbing the spiral staircase

Keys ready for the deadbolt

There is a pizza door hanger on the knob

It is for Mojo's Pizza

Grab it

Catch the special you can't miss it

In bold blocky Orange letters it advertises

Buy two Jumbo Jambalaya Creole Pizzas

Get a free Jarritos Orange Crush Six-Pack

Mandarin Orange Jarritos

Orange

Orange again

Sorry

911 will have to wait

Oblivious Morning Reflection

———

It is November 15, 1997 7:21 AM

There is an empty Mojo's Pizza box in the trash can

A non-empty pizza box in the recently plugged in mini fridge

This is the last day in New Orleans

Soon to be heading back home to Baltimore

Would be nice to make good use of the morning light

For filming check the walkman two more songs left to do

Maybe take a short drive

Revisit

And get another shot recorded

About to check out of the motel keys at the counter

Oh wait U-turn

Back to room 113

The other pizza!

Now back at the counter you check out of the motel

Dropping the keys off through the slot

The truck is already packed up

With typewriter knapsack odds-n-ends

It is a short drive to the New Orleans Museum of Art

The grounds of NOMA are gorgeous

There are plenty of trees

A reflecting pool with geese

Manicured lawns and a garden of delights

It is The Sydney and Walda Besthoff Sculpture Garden

Home to 55 sculptures by artists from around the world

As you stroll around these grounds

A discovery of a small pond under a bridge

Some geese have settled over there in the water

There is a song on the walkman titled

Oblivious Morning Reflection

Where this scene would fit perfectly

No fancy filter needed or required here

To document this scene in nature

Everything is synched up to record the geese in the pond

While putting the camcorder away you notice

There are clumps of Spanish moss laying on the ground

Wouldn't this stuff look pretty cool back at the pad?

Added to the nature scene in the bedroom?

I can see it I can see it no really

It's too sunny in there anyway

The plants prevented proper curtains drapes and privacy

And there is a need for less UV

A natural fit into the artist's statement

If there was one

So more pieces

Many more pieces of Spanish moss

Tossed into the bed liner of the truck

Put the camcorder in the knapsack

Which is weighed down by a brick

It is November 15, 1997 10:23 AM

After the morning stroll through the grounds

The time has finally come

Staying in New Orleans forever is not an option

It's time to begin the long journey back to Baltimore

Cold pizza to munch laying on the passenger seat

Last bottle of Jarritos

It is time to go

...72 miles...

...one year...

...418 miles...

...that felt kind of weird...

...511 miles...

...two years...

...716 miles...

...757 miles...

...three years...

...what's up with that?

...years?

...really?

...four years...

...904 miles...

...five years...

...1082 miles...

...six years...

...Whoa...what a strange trip...

...1117 miles...

I see it

Indigo baby!

Six years

Indigo

Well beyond November 1997

Did you know Two Thousand Three was also Indigo and—-

What's that?

Losing interest in baseball trivia?

You're right we did this one earlier

Used-Up Tiki Torches

September 23, 2003 4:30 PM

Well

These driving transitions are not going well

Here we are back in Baltimore but

Six years later and 15 miles north of the city

So go ahead you can park the tru—

Uh

Go ahead you can park the Brown Dodge Mini-van

Here we are back again in the suburbs

At Casa Des Arachnid

Your old roommate Jan is long gone

Jack put the house up for sale

The spiders take up residence back inside

The mini-van is packed full of moving boxes

Which just happen to be your worldly possessions

This van belongs to your friend Keeve

He lent it to you for the move

So climb up the stairs the front door is locked

The key can be slid through the mail slot

Look longingly through the front bay window

One last time

A baby grand piano that was never played

A fireplace that was once the key selling point

Never fired

You didn't live here long enough

For it to get cold enough to use

The house is still vacant

Turn around glance down at the friendly street

Ending in a tranquil cul-de-sac

Listen to the gentle stream trickling

That runs behind the house

A few crickets chirping

Walking to the backyard and patio to find

A barbeque grill laying on its side

No more ka-bobs

Burned out citronella candle buckets

Now full of maple leaves and rainwater

Used-Up Tiki Torches

Won't be burning those anymore

It's a new scene you're living back downtown now

No more roommates

Alone in a one bedroom

More action more people in the mix on the street

Or so it seems

Back downtown

More crime pollution rats in the alleys

It's not a long drive either

..10 minutes...

..20 minutes...

...see told ya we're here...

It is the Mt Vernon Apartment Building

After parking the mini-van

And unpacking one small light legal box

Time to walk upstairs and unlock it with apprehension

Air it out

Was that a mouse?

Climb the precariously stepped stairs

As most of the bulbs are burned out

Hopefully this key the landlord gave you fits

I'm sure it will give you fits

Well here you are it is home

A dingy third floor one bedroom apartment

Before you go back downstairs to unload the van

Take a break

What is in the box?

Find something sharp in the apartment

To cut the packing tape open with

Shake the box a bit and it sounds like

Knick-knacks inside rattling around

Try the kitchen for something sharp

A rather dull looking steak knife next to some dead cockroaches

Then another and another

And some of their undead brethren scurrying

The knife was just laying in a rotted old kitchen drawer

Slicing through the lid and packaging foam

A bunch of familiar well traveled goodies inside

Here is a small snow globe

No Santa instead of snow it contains gold sparkles

There is an outstretched hand

And a plaque under the hand that says

LOVE - FORTUNE - LUCK

Keep digging grab the candle

After examining more closely it isn't a Virgin Mary candle

It is St Jude Tadeo

There is a prayer on the back :

PRAYER TO ST. JUDE

Most holy apostle St Jude faithful servant and friend of Jesus

Patron of hopeless cases of things almost despaired of

Pray for me

I am so helpless and alone

Make use I implore you

Of that particular privilege given to you

To bring visible and speedy help

To where help is almost despaired of

I promise to be ever mindful of this great favor

To always honor you as my special

And most powerful patron

Amen

There is plenty more in the box

A single dried rose and it looks very old

The petals are extremely brittle and brown

Yet strong enough since most of the rose

Is still intact

Don't you remember?

Really the rose?

It was the girl from Tampa what's her name?

You went to the Rodan exhibit at The Met

Picasso's blue period

Georgia's cattle skulls

Paul Klee

That's when you gave her that rose

Later

She forgot to pack it on the way to the airport

Dig deeper into the box

These are crocheted doilies not made by a machine

But handmade

A large purple one made of thick yarn

Several others are black and made from thin thread

I have to ask I'm a bit curious

Conquests?

Trophies?

Keep going you haven't fished out all the prizes yet

There are several tubes of incense

Mmmm smells like an open box of frankincense

Small decanters of jasmine and sandalwood

Nice but

Come on something big and heavy at the bottom

Weighing the box down here we go

One filthy marble brick of rubble

From Saint Louis Cemetery #1

Yes it's that damn brick

That DAMN BRICK

You pick up the brick looking for a new fireplace mantel

And

Cut

Your Bizarre Fascination With Spanish Moss

———

And

Action

You pick up the brick from the fireplace mantel

And place it on the AC cord of the heat rock

There

That will weigh it down enough

So that Vinny can run around and it won't come unplugged again

It is November 15, 1998 4:16 PM

After that electric shock you are pleased with the solution

The brick will keep that heat rock from sliding around

And besides it will give Vinny another place

To hang out and scoot around in the cage

Of course that big trash bag of greenery from Savannah

Still sits in the middle of the living room floor

It is time to decorate

And acknowledge

Your Bizarre Fascination With Spanish Moss

The trash bag is completely full of it

Some sugar magnolia pine cones palm branches

Remove and dispose of whatever straggly withered mess laid before

Stayed clinging and adorning your gardens

Replace some moss on the ficus

Like hanging tinsel on a Christmas tree

It drapes around and falls to the floor

Very artsy

Reach up and intertwine some moss to the vines

Of the philodendron

It will help to obscure even more of the glass blown windows

Creating more privacy

Pull out some sugar magnolia leaves palm branches pine cones

And decorate the aquarium

The frogs don't seem to mind

The place looks more like a bayou swamp instead of Baltimore

There are no blinds curtains drapes in the window

Not that you could reach them anyway

These hanging plants spider plants ferns philodendron

Are enormous and their vines extend all the way to the ground

In the aquarium is a dry area where a hermit crab craws around

The soil is very moist and the moss helps keep it that way

Most of the old Spanish moss is pale and withered

All will be discarded

It is now November 15, 1998 6:05 PM

All of this decorating beautifying adorning is tiring

Maybe taking another short nap before dinner

To complete the transformation of your miniature Forsyth Park

Just a short nap

November 15, 1998

November 15, 1999

November 15, 2000

November 15, 2001

Eggs

November 15, 2001 6:00 PM

Well Rip Van Winkle that was quite a nap

Awakening in the master bedroom

Of the 30th street apartment

Exactly three years after decorating the room

Speaking of the room

The plants are gone

And the aquarium

And the trees

Better check on the iguana cage

Well Vinny is still there in the bottom of the tank

Though he doesn't look that good

There are several small stones next to him

Wait a second

Those aren't small stones

Those are eggs

Eggs

Definitely not Fabergé eggs

I guess Vinny is a girl

The iguana is lying limp and cold with eyes barely open

Laying eggs must have taken a toll on him/her

Don't you recall several years ago

Bringing the reptile into its new home

And it constantly escaping its enclosures

Till that one fateful Sunday

When it was sunning on the fire escape

And moments after your discovery of this

One false move and the reptile darted

Fell four stories to the concrete patio below

Peering down from the fire escape

Seeing its greenness shake and shudder

In counter-clockwise semicircle until ceasing

Descending down the spiral staircase in dismay

Expecting to retrieve a dismembered reptile

However

A twist of fate

Vinny would be fine and returned to his cage

Thirty minutes later munching romaine

Nature has a way of rewarding animals

With bad balance and vision

A pliable resilient body armored to survive awkward falls

This was the case as he slurped cantaloupe juice

Today though

Something is wrong something is different

The dark shriveled eggs absent of life

Picking up Vinny Greenballs and discovering

He/She is very cold

Perhaps some food will do the trick

You grab many different foods from the fridge

A few pieces of romaine lettuce

A couple slices of cantaloupe

Savoy spinach leaves

Try just a little piece of spinach

Even Popeye needed his

Vinny flicks the tongue out

Come on little green dude snap out of it

Perhaps some romaine lettuce to perk up

Vinny glances up meekly

Some of the cantaloupe just a little piece

A couple drops of cantaloupe juice on the tongue

Not much of a response

Keep trying

Romaine Cantaloupe Spinach

Spinach Romaine Cantaloupe

Cantaloupe Spinach Romaine

November 15, 2001 evening

Finally

Sadly

The realization that all hope is lost

Vinny Greenballs passes away

Vinny was six years old

RIP

After the death of Vinny spirits are at a new low

So go climb up the fire escape

Catch some air on the roof take a breather

Look up into the Baltimore skyline

A calming place of reflection in the past

It is a beautiful night sky actually

A cloudless day and now a full moon illuminates the roof

A small round black object poking out of the tar

Catches your eye

It is a lens cap for a camcorder

That must be about 5 years old

And has partially melted into the roofing tar

Grabbing on tight the lens cap becomes dislodged

While falling backwards

And bang your head on an exhaust vent

Camera model number 1 9 r e d 9 1

K. V.

While falling backwards banging your head on a heater vent

The lens cap becomes dislodged

From the door jam of the bookstore

Picked up and reattached to the camcorder

Still don't remember?

You recently finished filming around the campus

Of the University of Washington in Seattle

It is August 27, 1991 9:35 AM

Inside AKA Books across the street from Roxy Music Records

Located on the corner of University and NE 42nd Avenue

There are a handful of bicycles chained up

The store is rather busy

There is a rather ugly gray Ford Econoline Van parked in front

There are band flyers stapled to a telephone pole

One says The Lollapalooza Festival has been rescheduled

Momentary heartbreak

Oh it's just pushed ahead by one day

Originally for August 27 it will now be on Wednesday

August 28, 1991 at 12PM

Enumclaw park

Rain or shine

So this is really great news

More time to prepare for the show and do more sightseeing

Another day to kick around Seattle and find something to do

So stroll around in the store a bit

Another band flyer :

L7

ATOMIC 61

WOOL

DUMBHEAD

OFFRAMP

SEATTLE

AUG.27 8PM

Sounds like a night of sweet grunge

L7 from LA

Their big hit Shove appears on the Sub-Pop Grunge Years sampler

Who knows maybe the Butthole Surfers will show up

The night before their show in Enumclaw

With Lollapalooza that's a dozen bands in 24 hours

Now at the checkout counter of AKA books

There are a few people standing in line

By looking at the clerks nametag

His name is Eli

There is a rack of Just In Bargain Paperbacks nearby

One of these books catches your eye

White cover single Justin boot with flames

The title of the book is Bluebeard

Written by Kurt Vonnegut

While sifting through the bargain bin you spy another shopper

A rather attractive brunette who returns the glance

She is carrying a copy of

Pillars Of The Earth by Ken Follett to the checkout line

She smiles and looks away

Proceeds to the checkout counter

She pays for her book and leaves

As she strolls along

Eli waves to her exiting and says

See you later wonder girl!

May I help you sir?

Just this Kurt Vonnegut book

Kurt Vonnegut I heard this is a great one

Cool

Say do you know anything about the Lollapalooza Festival?

Well yes it is tomorrow and I'm going

Would you happen to know where Enumclaw Park is?

I guess you're not from around here

I'm just in town for the festival

A bunch of friends are meeting me here tomorrow

You can follow us

Thanks I'll see you tomorrow

Pay for the book and hastily exit the store

Nope

No wonder girl loitering outside

Not waiting on you man she's long gone

It is August 27, 1991 10:43 AM

Back to the GEO Metro rental car

Trolling around the Emerald City for an extra day

The Space Needle

The King Dome

Four innings of a Seattle Mariners game featuring Ken Griffey Jr

Puget Sound

Vashon Island

Athens Georgia

...???.... what?...

...road sign : "Welcome to South Carolina"...

19orange97

Seven Fifteen

April 8th, 1974

Atlanta Fulton County Stadium

Bernard Haywood and his nephew

Henri Edson Ximenez

Have seats in the bleachers to watch the game between

The Los Angeles Dodgers and The Atlanta Braves

Henry Aaron number 44 for the home team

Has hit 714 homeruns over the course of his career

Tied for first all-time with the legendary Babe Ruth

Bernard spent two weeks pay for tickets bus a motel room

Got some time off from the Memphis MLGW

Both Henri-y-s in attendance Lonnie watching from above

As number 44 cracks number 715 and breaks the record

Seven Fifteen

Henri will turn seventeen this summer

He will also get a job with MLGW as a security intern

Bernard had married a year earlier

Juanita originally from Kentucky

She used to sing for a doo-wop band called The Black Sirens

And for the first time

Henri was happy at home

Bernard and Juanita took the place of his parents

With no arguing bickering

They treated him like the young adult he was

Henri did not want to attend college

And there was no pressure from his step-parents to do so

He wanted to follow the success of Bernard

At MLGW

He worked his way up to an assistant security head

Made good money good bonuses

Moved out of the house by nineteen to a sunny apartment

Not far from the old homestead pretty close to Beale Street

It seems he was given a taste of Stax and Sun records

That his father Lonnie once dreamed of when he was that age

In his early twenties

He became a regular at all the great clubs in Memphis

Blues City Cafe

Band Box

BB Kings Blues club

Automatic Slims

As the 1970s turned into the 1980s

Henri had worked his way up the ranks of the power company

A top lieutenant in security

Bernard Haywood had retired by then

He and Juanita were still happily settled in the same house

Not far from his nephew

By the 1990s Henri had become head of security

At MLGW

He never married

He started following the Memphis Tigers basketball team

And would take his uncle to games at The Pyramid

The big NCAA college tournament venue

One night he headed to his uncles house

For a big season opener versus Vanderbilt

But when he arrived

Juanita was in tears

Turns out her mother had passed away

In Kentucky

With Juanita and her husband distraught

Henri volunteered to safely drive the family

To Louisville for the funeral

The date of the service is November 11, 1997

And the service was to be held at

The Church Of The Holy Name

Georgia

Darkness

Driving

On the highway near the Georgia - South Carolina border

Late approaching midnight

It is November 15, 1997 11:30 PM

Sitting in the 1987 Nissan pickup still tick-tick-ticking

En route to Baltimore departed New Orleans earlier

This is Interstate I-85 northbound somewhere near the border

Of Georgia and South Carolina

The organ music cassette is now in the trucks tape deck

Listen

This particular instrumental may be the best

The piece is called Tears Reflected In Taillights

Hmmm the camcorder is nearby and ready

Look into oncoming traffic the lonely headlights of other travelers

They're heading southbound late at night across the median

Red tail lights in front of you jersey wall to left

This would make a cool shot

See if the camcorder can be placed on the dashboard

Record the cars coming in the other direction

Carefully

Synch up the music from the walkman to the camcorder

And begin recording

The headlights of oncoming traffic to I-85 white light

White Light

White Heat

It is November 15, 1997 11:57 PM

This recording is the final one for the music video

All tracks of organ music that you recorded a week earlier

Now have a corresponding video representation

Mission accomplished

And excitement

To carry you back home to Baltimore

There you will start editing the project

Into a short video presentation complete with chapters

But there are still many more miles to reach Baltimore

Now somewhere in the state of South Carolina

Glance in the rearview mirror at all the oddities

Stored in the bed liner including

Plenty of Spanish moss

Sugar magnolia leaves

186

Palm tree branches

And a brick

External Ventilation

———

Kimberly Deirdre Logan

The mother of Juanita Logan is laid to rest

Henri and Bernard were two of the pall bearers

Both men in beautiful black Perry Ellis suits

Bernard glancing over at his nephew

Thinking about how far he has come

A sickly looking child awkward at baseball

Now taking control of this situation

A head honcho at the power company

Going far beyond the pay grade that Bernard once held

He was extremely proud

And in a moment of reflection

Knew

That his sister Dorothea

RIP

Would have been proud of the son she hardly knew

Henri had different things on his mind as he carried the casket

Remembering to check the oil in the Pontiac Bonneville

Add air to the passenger rear tire which had a slow leak

So it could make it safely back to Memphis

Also lost in thought

Trying to figure out a sensible way

To approach Bernard about help with a gambling debt

He was being followed around Memphis

By the lowlifes who needed the debt paid back quick

The Memphis Mob

Too much betting on the NCAA basketball games

Memphis Light Gas & Water also knew about this

It was only a matter of time before he would lose his career

All these things weighed on Henri much more than the casket

When out of the corner of his eye

He spied a young man

Out of time and place

He was walking up the steps Miss Logan was just carried out of

Holding a camcorder

Not quite sure what he was recording

Or who he could have been spying on

After the service

The family drove immediately back to Memphis

Henri dropped Bernard and Juanita off

A big heartfelt hug from each

Way to stand up Henri you pulled us through

Mission Accomplished

Henri had other things to do

MLGW granted him bereavement time for the funeral

But they had an urgent matter they needed to discuss with him

Henri knew what was going on

He knew all about the urgent matter

You needed to have a spotless record to stay in security

No booze drugs felonies or even unsavory gambling debts

It would be a series of meetings that would last all afternoon

During a break from these discussions regarding

Severance pension suspension paid time off

He returned to his security console

Made a cup of coffee

Glad Bernard and Juanita were settled back home

No

He wouldn't drag his uncle into this gambling mess

Maybe he would explain he was given a vacation

Maybe Florida Mississippi or The Big Easy

After a second cup

He tried to focus on the monitors

To distract from the hot water he was in

Monitor 1 Turbine vane -1.3 per cycle

Monitor 2 Incinerator .04 above carbon PPSI

Monitor 3 Technicians working electrical generator

Monitor 4 External Ventilation for trans shaft BE-5 walkway clear

Monitor 5 External Ventilation for trans shaft AF-5 walkway not

Monitor 6 External Ventilation a huge flock of blackbirds—-

External Ventilation a huge flock—-

A huge flock of wait a minute

Wait

No

No

No it can't possibly be

That guy from the funeral service it can't

Zooming in on Monitor 6

Zoom

In closer

Zoom in tight

No

No way

...

...

...

We have confirmation

A Rainbow On Top

———

...1 9 r e d 9 1...

...1 9 o r a n g e 9 7...

...1 9 y e l l o w 9 8...

...2 0 g r e e n 0 1...

...2 0 b l u e 0 2...

...2 0 i n d i g o 0 3...

...2 0 v i o l e t 0 4...

That chronology

Along with that one and only color scheme

That is on the computer screen

Along with a rainbow image you photo-shopped

A Rainbow On Top

Something a leprechaun conspired with

Neither end in sight

Anyway

You were sitting at your computer and briefly nodded out

It is October 19, 2004 11:45PM

In the bedroom of the Mt Vernon apartment

Minimize the rainbow image maximize another window

This appears to be a transcript from an MSN Messenger chat :

10/19/2004 11:42:33 PM you Octoberiffic I drove it a little bit
has a quiet engine

10/19/2004 11:42:56 PM you Octoberiffic I was sick of the Camry anyway

10/19/2004 11:43:08 PM you Octoberiffic by the end of the year I'll know

10/19/2004 11:43:15 PM you Octoberiffic ;)

10/19/2004 11:43:55 PM you Octoberiffic I'll give Steve the money tomorrow

10/19/2004 11:45:16 PM Octoberiffic you ??????????????

10/19/2004 11:45:35 PM Octoberiffic you What kind of van is it?

10/19/2004 11:45:38 PM you Octoberiffic A Ford Econoline like Eli's

10/19/2004 11:45:45 PM you Octoberiffic Carpenters like them because
you can fit an entire 9 foot bolt of carpet in and still close the rear doors

10/19/2004 11:45:53 PM you Octoberiffic Great touring vans

10/19/2004 11:46:05 PM Octoberiffic you So I'm halfway through
BOOK ONE

10/19/2004 11:46:19 PM Octoberiffic you love the Lollapalooza part :)

10/19/2004 11:51:51 PM you Octoberiffic Funny...almost done
BOOK TWO

10/19/2004 11:53:48 PM Octoberiffic wow
I can't wait to read it

10/19/2004 11:54:10 PM you Octoberiffic pretty soon might just
hand it to you

10/19/2004 11:54:14 PM you Octoberiffic ...

10/19/2004 11:54:42 PM you Octoberiffic :)

10/13/2004 11:54:57 PM you Octoberiffic l8tr tater

10/13/2004 11:56:59 PM Octoberiffic you oh ya?

10/13/2004 11:57:14 PM Octoberiffic you does it end happily?

10/13/2004 11:57:24 PM Octoberiffic you I'm assuming it will :}

10/13/2004 11:57:43 PM you Octoberiffic perhaps

10/13/2004 11:58:03 PM you Octoberiffic If I do depart
I will pass through The Big N.O.

10/13/2004 11:58:20 PM Octoberiffic you The Big Easy?

10/13/2004 11:58:24 PM you Octoberiffic Of course...

.

10/13/2004 11:58:33 PM you Octoberiffic ...and I'll be bringing
a BRICK with me

10/13/2004 11:58:41 PM you Octoberiffic later WNDGRL

A few more changes are made to BOOK TWO

Review the typing for spelling errors

Add the file as an attachment

And finally

Press SEND

Garnet Red And Bondo

———

There was still enough gas in the Bonneville

Even after the long drive from Louisville

For Henri to hop in and chase the man down in the parking lot

Nope too late

He did manage to see the burgundy Nissan truck

It had Maryland plates

I guess the man knew his cover was blown because he headed west

Across the Mississippi River

To Arkansas

This was turning into the kind of security detail that Henri

The kind of excitement

That Henri dreamed would be commonplace

Envisioning his heroics

Instead

Most often just trying to stay awake

While staring at monitors all shift

Both vehicles cross from Tennessee into Arkansas

The truck takes the first exit to a motel

Completely oblivious to the tail

Henri followed

Deftly shadowing his prey but not too closely

At the motel counter

The man leaves the office carrying a blue American Tourister

He reports to room 0 4

Henri studied him

I don't get it

Did the Memphis Mob call the ringer in from out of state?

Why Maryland?

The troubles at MLGW were resolvable

A few months unpaid leave and they would have him back

The Memphis Mob was another thing

So Henri took a room under an alias

Across the lot he is in 0 5

Spyglass under the curtains

No movement it's getting dark

Then

Another vehicle pulls up

Well I'll be

It's a 1972 Mercury Marquis

Yup

The Mercury Marquis Brougham Edition

The Ford 460 big block

222 horsepower

Garnet Red And Bondo

The pimp car of the mob

It pulls slowly across crushing gravel

Parks in front of 0 6 next to the truck

Well

The headlights go off but the engine still idles

You cannot miss those headers

That glass pack exhaust growl

A few minutes pass and the Mercury shuts off

Nobody moves

Apparently the driver is just going to kick it

Why rent a motel room

When the backseat of the Brougham Edition is more comfortable

He exits the drivers door

And checks into the rear door and back seat for the night

The night turns into the following morning

At dawn

The man in room 0 4 awakens refreshed

A tired man in 0 5 eating motel cheese-its to stay mostly awake

A zonked out man in front of 0 6

Sprawled on the roomy back seat of the Mercury

Brougham Edition

He waits to hear the Nissan ignition before arising

Tick-tick-ticking

Damn homey cross-threaded a spark plug

It is now November 12, 1997 early AM

The Nissan truck checks out of the motel first

Unsuspectingly followed by a Pontiac Bonneville

And then the Mercury Marquis

Brougham Edition

Forms the caboose

The trio cross the bridge back into Tennessee

Then hang a right turn onto interstate 55 South

Then it begins

A

Long

Relentless

Drive to New Orleans

The Nissan will make unwitting or unconcerned stops

Along the way

And also into and around New Orleans

Oblivious Morning Reflection that's no joke to this guy

The Bonneville stays cued onto the lead driver

Occasionally glancing into the rear view mirror

Puts flashers on double parks idles if necessary

The Brougham Edition is mostly just taking notes

With traffic getting trickier in the Quarter

The Bonneville has trouble shadowing the truck

Double parks again with the flashers

At Saint Louis Cemetery Number One

The Nissan parks for the final time

Henri Edson Ximenez

Has had enough of this game

If the mob wants to make an example of me so be it

He is a block away from the man from Maryland

Who is adjusting his camera

At the same time

The Memphis Mob has also had enough

The Brougham Edition

Punches all two hundred of its horses

Speeds on course for the Maryland man

Henri makes an instinctual decision

Guided through years of training in security

He pushes the Maryland man out of the way

The Brougham Edition

Disappears

Belches thick black smoke a hiccup of exhaust in its wake

Henri returns to the Pontiac

The man in the street is down but he is not out

After a few minutes he dusts himself off

Gets up grabs the camcorder and knapsack

Continues into the cemetery like nothing happened

Henri face-palms

Removes his other hand from the Bonneville steering wheel

Shrugs

Clicks opens the drivers door and resumes his mission

He is well aware of the opportunity

That the height of the cemetery walls created

The Great White Hope

My shoes have served you well

I wish to thank you traveler

For a job well done

Much like a 400 meter relay race

It is my turn now to take the baton

So we can cross the finish line

The rainbow you ran spanned thirteen years

I will pick this up beyond the rainbow

On January 3rd, 2005

I depart Baltimore headed south in a Ford van packed to the gills

Yup a Ford Econo-line carpenters van inspired by Eli's

It is white no bondo and my mother RIP renamed it

The Great White Hope

As in a boxer fighting against the odds

A stop for gas just south of Pamplin Park near Petersburg VA

After 406 tiring miles time to stop

At a rest area near Lexington North Carolina

By dusk a gas stop across the Georgia state line in Lavonia

Then thirty miles later a stop for dinner

At Commerce GA a factory outlet center north of Athens

Tonight it's a Chinese food buffet

Packed in Styrofoam and eaten at the drivers seat

Have to keep eyes close to the van at all times

It occurs to me now

Scarfing down the moo shu pork with plum sauce

That I will probably be eating alone for the rest of my life

As darkness falls I want to be west of Atlanta to avoid AM traffic

The motel room is in Douglasville GA

January 4th, 2005

Taking I-59 south of Tuscaloosa and route 11 through Foster

Just needed to get off the interstate for a while to clear the head

Approaching the Pearl River and the next stop is I-10 West

En route to New Orleans

Ok

Let me skip a bit further

There will be plenty of time to talk New Orleans

I want to save that for later

I need to get you past that

It is important

So here we go

Somewhere between Baton Rouge and Lake Charles

Lies the Atchafalaya Welcome Center

There was not a soul around

Yet there was a recorded history booming from loudspeakers

Surrounding the property

January 5th, 2005

After a night in Lake Charles

Creole catfish po-boy on crackers at midnight

Next morning

The steep on ramp back to I-10

The long drive through most of Texas

The first spots of rain near Columbus

Halfway between Houston and San Antonio

A beautiful garnet sunset near Sonora Texas

Then another motel in Fort Stockton

January 6th, 2005

The next stop for gas at Fabens about forty miles from El Paso

In the afternoon suddenly tired like day one

Pull over at a rest stop in Las Cruces New Mexico

Still just a brief stint of rain in Texas that was it

The van ran very well so far just added power steering fluid

Engine temp hot going uphill cool going down

Like Chuck Berry stated in Maybelline

Rolling into Tucson AZ Thursday at sunset

Checking the weather channel at a Motel 6

Two severe storms pounding

The entire pacific coast

Mudslides

One tomorrow morning and one on Sunday

Decide to take 3 days off sunning it up in Tucson

These three days working out the kinks

So the sciatica could calm down

Refreshing strolls about town

The baseball diamond with Mount Lemmon in the outfield

Plentiful orange trees abound

Though a four pound bag was just a buck

Catalina State Park on Sunday off Oracle road

Then back at the motel watching football

Michael Vick loses to the Eagles in the snow

Mind and cardio much clearer now

Ready to resume the mission

Monday morning January 10, 2005

By eleven AM sixty miles west of Phoenix

Prepared to deal with whatever remnants

Of those pacific storms still exist

With great fortune

California exit 107 I-40 arrives

To a burst of sunshine

Now the northern ascent through the Mojave desert

Finally seeing snow on the mountain peaks

This route skirts around San Bernadino County

And the Sierras

Gladly take route 58N through the dustbowl

For dry road conditions

Then it's route 99 in Bakersfield

Without question the longest drive past Fresno

A motel in Madera California its 3AM

Awake four hours later

A morning torrential rain and dreary drive to the I-580 west

As the worst traffic yet on this trip

Occurs near The Bay Bridge

A reward sighted in reflection to the east

Multi-colored light through a prism

A rainbow

A reminder of the manuscript started several months ago

And the mission of this voyage

A Rainbow On Top

Something a naughty leprechaun conspired with

Still neither end in sight

But we're getting close

Crossing the Benicia Martinez Bridge

And heading I-780 west to CA29

This will tour through the Napa Valley

The rain has stopped

It is past the wine counties of Napa Sonoma and Santa Rosa

Midday now it is route 101 traversing Humboldt County

Gas in Healdsburg California

With a destination of Eureka for dinner

While making Arcata and a food stop at 3:30

A road sign is spotted

Portland 397 miles

Damn

A miscalculation

Thought it would only be a couple hours left

Approaching Crescent City and rapidly losing sunlight

It was decision time on The Lost Coast

I went for it

Continuing on the 101 as night approaches

And a light misty rain starts to fall

Coos Bay Oregon

Hey buddy oh you're from out of state

There isn't self serve gas here

Ok gotcha

The last stop for gas

Tiring of the curvy and slow 101

A hard right turn at Reedsport Oregon

Making a mad dash east to I-5

Just south of Eugene Oregon

Then a hot couple hours north

Maximum speed approaching the I-205

And the suburban Portland counties

Finally the last leg is concluding

In the town of Gresham Oregon

Wednesday 1:15 AM

Exactly 19 hours since that last motel in California

I promise to get back to New Orleans

I do

There is just some more commentary

More that you need to hear first

It seems like a red carpet directed me to Portland

Before that week ended

I was employed

Before that month ended

I was in a house

With a car

Even the storage unit

The first month free was exactly that

Just had to pay for the lock

All these achievements in Portland

Seemed to somehow be connected

With the events that transpired in New Orleans

So now

This is what happened

I had a destination in the French Quarter

But I was in no hurry

I caught a bench to rest around the courtyard

Spying Jackson Square for a spell

Treated myself to Cafe Du Monde

Black coffee and beignets

Burned off the caffeine with a relaxing stroll

Through Louis Armstrong Park

One that I never fully completed previously

Then it was off to Saint Peter and Rampart streets

And Saint Louis Cemetery Number One

A different knapsack this time

The previous one was stolen

I remember the time it was 2:45 PM

I walked past the headless Peter Fonda statue again

We blew it Billy we blew it

No Wyatt we didn't blow it

It wouldn't be much trouble to remember

The tomb I needed to visit

J A Rousseau

The trick remembering was that

One of my favorite songs

In A Jar by the group Dinosaur Junior

Seven more years of rot and crumbling

It was tricky trying to match exactly

The white of the marble to the much filthier tomb

The reason was I had kept the brick clean

All those years

Indoors most of the time

I pulled it out of the bag

And returned it to its similar trim pieces

That same spot from 1997

Mission Accomplished

And at that exact moment

I heard footsteps

I was hardly surprised

Actually glad

No

It was not a cemetery tour guide

I turned around

And I was standing face to face

With none other than

Henri Edson Ximenez

Henri Edson Ximenez

You did it

You returned the brick

Not only that but when you returned the brick

I came back

I'm back baby!

In my body in my skin in my clothes

In my soul

The Perry Ellis still looks tight

Allow me to introduce myself

My name is Henri Edson Ximenez

Ring a bell?

You may have heard of me by my initials

H. E. Ximenez

That's right

I am your HEX

Human form obviously

You know it is hard to believe

But I once thought you were my ringer

You were coming after me for the hit

Ha Ha Ha

Nope

Just some tourist with a camera focusing on a church

An insipid tourist hanging around the grounds

Of my employment

Memphis Light Gas & Water

Finding blackbirds on a power line so inspiring photogenic

Just showing up at the wrong place at the right time

Twice

Not only was I confused

I shared my befuddlement with the Memphis Mob

I guess they thought you were my money man

Hmmm

That November afternoon in 97

The Mob had had enough

The sequence of events that followed are still confusing

Let me fill you in

The Brougham Edition punched it

All 222 horses

I managed to push you out of the way

I then ran back to my car

I thought you were down but not out

After a moment you dusted yourself off in the street

Incredibly nonchalantly

Like you were just bitten by a mosquito

Then you proceeded back into

Saint Louis Cemetery Number One

What the hell guy

Curiosity killed me

Literally I believed

I followed you in

Walked quietly past the tour group

Then watched you do something unusual

You removed a piece of marble rubble brick from a tomb

At that same moment

Everything changed for me

I was out of my body

I was floating

I couldn't feel my hands

Out of my skin my clothes my eyes

At that time I thought I knew what happened

It must have been when I pushed you aside

It was I who got run over by the Mob

I got hit by the car

I was the one who died

It brought sadness and peace at the same time

I imagined

MLGW

Would contact my uncle Bernard back in Memphis

Explain Henri had gambling debts

Believed the Mob tailed him down to New Orleans

Probably disposed of Henri's body in Lake Pontchartrain

Eventually eaten by nutrias

No body to recover

That of course wasn't the case

It was somehow much worse than that

I became imprisoned trapped in your mind

Stuck in your thoughts

At the strangest times

This odd man

This tourist

And you

As warden

You somehow fixated on the idea

Of a HEX for the next seven years

Seven ungodly years

Even when you put the brick in the truck initially

That fateful day

Almost immediately created doubt in your mind

On returning home

Everywhere the brick was placed brought misfortune

Could it be because you kept moving it?

You never stayed in one place long enough

The stupid brick

That insipid chunk of limestone

Always got packed into various odds and ends moving boxes

For every relocation you did

What a joke

Then when it came time to talk about it

To tell some other worldly entity of your HEX

You choose the counsel of your supposed flame

The one you had the hots for

Of course I'm talking about

The one and only

Ilsa Navas

This Thing you have for Ilsa Navas

Who explains that the evil spirits are pissed

What a hack job

What a line

From the tyro journalist

How many Jim and Gingers did you have?

You wormed the devastating 9-1-1 tragedy

Into this fateful mix as well

My goodness

Is everything that goes wrong in this world connected to you?

The bands record comes out that same day

You find touring depressing

Dull

Wow

I think you got some issues to work out buddy

You did finish the New Orleans video

Even stashed it at Video Americain

Which was the hipster Baltimore boutique for VHS

Plus you continued your music career

Several more musical collaborations

Created a website with all of your material

All in all this sounds very prolific

So why do you think you had a HEX?

Why did it only come out when you had doubt?

Then another move and another roommate

You burden Jan with the ordeal

And she thinks Jack is selling the house

Because of the HEX?

This is all too much for me

And the punch line

My goodness the punch line is believing

I had something to do

With an iguana leaping off a balcony

And then three years later

Turns up dead in its cage

With lifeless eggs resting next to the brick

It would be funny if it weren't so sad

Because you fought back against me

By writing about me in your first drafts

Didn't give me a proper name

Then you called this manuscript

Something About A HEX

Which you emailed to the Wonder Girl from Washington

I can tell you right now

That it's not going to work out with her

You're wasting your time

This voyage will take you to Portland

And no further

Oops spoiler alert

Sorry champ

But dammit

As soon as you pressed SEND on that draft

And you spoke the HEX into existence

I was stuck with you

So I hatched a plan

From then on

When there wasn't emptiness

Darkness

A void

Despair in my world

That my lifeless body could not escape from

The only kind of consciousness I observed

My only being

Was these deep seeded thoughts

Doubts

Disappointments

Delusions

In your mind

That I was a spell put onto you

A spell that would replay all the events

In this saga

Encapsulated over 13 years

From 1991 through 2004

Over and over again

In a different order each time

Randomly

As a remedy

As a solution for letting me go

It was my attempt

To cease and desist from your dark thoughts

So I could escape

To get you to bring that damn brick

Back to New Orleans

If it meant life death or peace for myself

At that point none of those mattered

I would settle for any of it

It was seven years of replaying all those events

With different scenarios

Like shuffling cards in a deck

Looking to pull out that ace

For example

You keep trying to play the keyboard without the right pedal

You cannot find the T-Shirt stand at the Lollapalooza Concert

Nor do you claim a will call ticket that gives you two

Jan has an endless supply of spiders that terrify her

You keep trolling churches in Louisville

Until you find the right funeral

You have to be in sight of the TV cameras

At Memphis Light Gas & Water

Ilsa Navas

She will continue to make excuses

That two Scorpios don't mix

Mortal Arthur telephones from random points of exile

Hafnarfjörður Quebec City Prince Edward Island

Ultimately Thule the northernmost city in the world

Subsisting on walrus fat and teaching Icelandic to Inuits

WNDRGRL continues to change her MSN chat name

From Octoberiffic to Pumpkinspies to Hallobean

Yes

I fought back in this mental prison nicely as well

When you got lost along the way

I made sure in the Seattle mosh pit

You always get a Doc Marten

Somewhere where a Doc Marten shouldn't be

The New Orleans Tarot reader

Randomly selects time and distance

Thought you knew that

I always make you miss the Link Wray show

I was tempted to have the black Corolla break down

But I liked that car it had style

So I kept trashing the Camry instead

Too many Jim and Gingers at Dougherty's

Just barely missing the DUI

Only because I needed you to keep driving

And the coup de grace

All that Spanish Moss

I kept whispering in your ear

I don't think you have enough

Not nearly enough

Keep bending over scoop up some more

More

More

Ha

Vinny always dies

It's a reptile that's what they do

At the bookstore in Seattle

The girl always smiles at you

Just like a reptile

That's what they do

I did mix up the Vonnegut selections

Sometimes Bluebeard sometimes Mother Night

Occasionally Breakfast Of Champions

Yes

All of this hoping that one day

You would get the nerve to pack your things

Draw up a one way trip

To the Pacific Northwest

And most importantly

Bring the damn brick with you

Travel back south through The Big N.O.

Return it to it's eternal resting place

Maybe that is the only way

I can get out of this loop

Take my chances with whatever comes next

Because enough of you

Now it is time

I'm back!

Being back in my clothes feeling quite refreshed

I can get on a bus

I can go back to Memphis

Tell Bernard and Juanita

I got scared

I had to stay away

So that the mob wouldn't visit you

Talk to Memphis Light Gas & Water

They would take me back

So here we are

Today

I've waited a long time for you to figure this all out

To tell me what the hell a HEX is

So here I am

Pardon the excessive curiosity but

You owe it to me

Tell me all about it

If It Takes The Form Of A Human

———

You are not what I imagined

You are better

You are much more inventive than what I imagined

You worried the lines for a better fit

To match the fit of your suit

This has been an exercise in memory

For both of us

Though the truth is much more damning than that

Through our supposed years together

You have been on my mind

But not exactly

The truth

Henri

Is that you do not exist

As I revisited the story I wrote

Over twenty years ago

Something About A Hex

I had this nagging feeling that it was not resolved

There was a certain incompleteness to it

The alleged HEX had no voice

No motive

No intelligence

No debate

No response

So I created you

I needed a physical representation

Of what was living in my mind

To take the form of a human

Barely living

Just in recall answering ever so occasionally

Yet

What was there needed to be removed for good

Let's get started have a seat

Your grandfather

Eliades Ximenez

Well I am a big fan of Eliades Ochoa

The guitarist from the Buena Vista Social Club

He also has a band called Afro-Cubism

Where he collaborates with musicians from Mali

I saw him in concert once with Afro-Cubism

Though he didn't perform his most famous tune that night

El Carretero

The Cart Man

You can see him perform that song

Walking along the train tracks of Cuba

In the film Buena Vista Social Club

Your middle name

Edson

I did have you share the same birthday

With this influential figure the great guitarist

Edson Lopes

He is Brazilian

I enjoy his classical depictions of Bach and Scarlatti

Your surname Ximenez is of Spanish origin

So you see

You cannot connect all of these dots

Cuba

Brazil

Spain

I liked the name Lonnie for your father

It fit well in establishing the baseball connection

Back in the early 1980s there was a flash on the diamond

His name was Lonnie Smith

He helped three different teams win a World Series

I cannot explain Dorothea

Nor was I comfortable in her distance from you

Maybe it derived from the Wizard Of Oz Dorothy

I'm not sure

I am sure of her and Bernard's last name

I chose the name Haywood from someone I respected

You weren't a blue baby

I was

The baseball stuff well

Let's just say we shared similar experiences

You were taken on trips from Chicago to Milwaukee

Just to see Henry Aaron play

It wasn't Bernard and Lonnie sneaking into the stadium

It was my father and his cousin Charles that hopped the fence

To see The Baltimore Orioles play back in '54

Lonnie wanted the name Henry obviously

Dorothea demanded the I at the end not Y

To remind her of the French hypnotist she studied

Grandpa came from Metairie

Close enough to the cemetery where this drama began

He relocated himself and Lonnie to Seattle

Where I would one day set foot for Lollapalooza

Then the move to Chicago for the blues

Where you would be born

Which was also the train hub for the Seattle trip

Louisville

Memphis

I put both of our stamps there

It's over

You don't have to get on a bus to Memphis

The people you knew there do not exist

So your journey ends here

Though we never became friends

I want to thank you

I could not overcome the lingering of a hex

That I could not see

It will take twenty years into the future

To write you back into time

Only when the HEX

Took the form of a human

Could I see and understand it

That there was indeed no HEX at all

I needed to hear it

I needed you to tell me

You were pulling my strings

Eventually we would meet

And I would pull yours

With this information I knew

If It Takes The Form Of A Human

I'll Kick It's Ass

So traveler

I suddenly found myself alone in a cemetery

As

Henri Edson Ximenez

Disappeared into thin air

I learned a lot from Henri

Mostly how we live in the past present and future

As our three lives meet here

Simultaneous with our thoughts

In a revaluation of determining influence

The HEX disappeared as soon as I arrived in Portland

Just a week after the return of the brick to New Orleans

The brick was no more

The HEX was no more

And Henri is no more

And this story is it's official conclusion

I was reinvigorated then and also now

Remembering that my true life advisors

Would always be with me in my thoughts

Amplified focused and at my disposal

With the HEX removed altogether

These two trusted sources to seek counsel

For important decisions advice and answers

Even if left to the imagination

These two I sought counsel from

My mother Giovanna

My father John Granville

They guided me along the way

Even after their passing

I still look above to them for their grace

I conclude with one admission

Connected to the opening of this story

Henri made some important notes

He explained

You cannot accept more from me than memory

You cannot expect more from memory than this

I may want to rephrase those just a tad

All we are is our memories

He also said

This is not Jesus

No it is not

Maybe

Just maybe

He got that one wrong too

I was going to tell him a story

A story about Jesus

He did in fact say

Tell me all about it

But I decided against it

It goes something like this

Jesus Lived Beneath The House

———

I'm driving to Annapolis Maryland

From Baltimore City on a sunny day

I'm approaching a bridge over water

Which doesn't exist in the route

The traffic backs up and a freeway alert sign suggests

To park our cars and walk on the bridge

So I park my car in Fells Point

Which is actually located in the Baltimore Inner Harbor

I park the car on Greenwich Street which isn't there either

And now I'm walking back to the highway to cross the bridge

Walking and talking with a crowd that gets bigger

And bigger

Now we see the problem

We are approaching a raised drawbridge that is stuck

I tell the people to stay away from the railing of this bridge

It is simply a galvanized coil chain and not too stable

Suddenly a tugboat bumps into the bridge

The vibration causes several people to lose balance

They fall into the water

I urge the rest of them to stay away because it could happen again

I am standing near the railing now

Talking with three young girls

From Junior High school I once knew

One of them asks me to go downstairs with her

To make out

I look for a stairway off of this bridge

We find and take some stairs down underneath the bridge

Which opens into some damp dank warehouse

Motorcycle parts strewn about

It is barely lit with water and motor oil on the floor

Predominately a dark blue hue from a buzzing fluorescent light

I can now hear cars overhead where there once were pedestrians

I start to make out with this girl

When one of her friends runs downstairs and says

Hey the bridge is down and everyone is moving let's go

We head back upstairs

The bridge asphalt is now withered yellow grass

Also it is now night and there are lights illuminating

What appears to be a racetrack

It is an amateur stock car race

Where cars are racing one at a time

Time trials

To see if they qualify to be professional race car drivers

Or amateur race car drivers

A friend with Thick Eyeglasses is on the course

Driving a Plymouth blue and red

Running his final lap

At the end of the race the crowd votes

To determine who are the professional and amateur drivers

Thick Eyeglasses is voted professional

His prize is to drive his stock car inside a Kmart department store

There he can fill the stock car

With as much merchandise as he chooses

His car is now inside the brightly lit Kmart

Doing burnouts on the tile

He has filled the car with mostly fishing poles

Which stick out of the windows on each side

A Babe Ruth Bobble-head on rear dash

With the race now over

People are leaving and I am joined by Thick Eyeglasses

A mysterious woman who closely resembles the actress

Lauren Hutton

And her Handsome Male Companion

I am immediately attracted to her pretty blue eyes

Guess her age to be late thirties forties

I tell her I need a ride back to my car

That I parked back in Fells Point

The four of us are in their car

It is an orange early 70's AMC Javelin

We get in Handsome Male Companion is driving

Thick Eyeglasses is riding shotgun

She and I are in the backseat

There is no floor in the car bare metal with rusted holes

We're driving back to my car

When we notice

All these various graveyards

That we have to keep detouring around

The graveyards are separated by locks of water

Similar to the ones at the C&O Canal near Georgetown in DC

I tell Handsome Male Companion to be careful

As we are weaving around tombstones

And I don't want the car to swerve into one of these locks

I ask the woman how old she is

Seventy Five she says

Many too many facelifts keeping her young

She laughs Handsome Male Companion and her together

For two years now celebrating their garnet wedding anniversary

Handsome Male Companion smashes the car into a tombstone

Thick Eyeglasses is ejected through the windshield

She and I get out

She says we are now going to visit the house I grew up in

She tells me the tomb where Jesus died is buried under my house

Jesus Lived Beneath The House

We enter my house which is a red brick colonial

They have installed an elevator on the first floor

Which goes down one level to the basement

Then one more level to the tomb in the sub floor

We get on the elevator and go down to the basement

There is a closed-circuit viewer showing the tomb beneath us

The tomb is called Montmartre The Place Where Jesus Died

There is music playing in the tomb I can hear through the floor

It is Chopin's Prelude 4

I heard that once in Five Easy Pieces

Played by Jack Nicholson

For Susan Anspach

On a loop

I am joined by my brother and sister

My brother asks me

What type of speakers am I using for my home stereo

I reply two Tannoy studio monitors and two Polk fours

I ask him if he is going beneath to see the tomb

He says that he is not interested

I start to cry

I ask my sister if she will go downstairs with me

To Montmartre the place where Jesus died

She also declines

I start getting nauseous and continue crying

I head to the basement bathroom near the elevator towards the tomb

It looks exactly as it did in the 1970s

Part of an unfinished club basement

Paneling cement floor partial tile throw rugs

Just a commode sink and laundry hamper no shower

The same as it was when I was growing up

I look in the bathroom mirror

I'm noticing my tears resemble saliva

There are little bubbles in them

The fluid is really gooey and white

I start to spit in the sink and then I start vomiting

The vomit comes out really dry

As if it is tied to one continuous string

It looks as if there are munched up

Crackers chips cookies all sch-mooshed together

Like a Chunky Bar extraction from a cadavers throat

External Ventilation

Also known as breathing

I continue over to the toilet

Trying to expel the matter

Grabbing the vomit rope and start tugging on it

All twisting like a vine like a philodendron

Pulling it out of my throat with my bare hands

Reaching over for a scissors

That were miraculously placed there on the toilet lid

Trying to cut the vine

Then

Conscious

That was Jesus

Yes it was